ANIMAL ZOO

ANIMAL ZOO

ORSO MARRONE

OMF
PUBLISHING

ISBN 979-8-9901820-9-7

Cover/Interior Book Design: Steve May

Cover Art: Barry Brown

Orso Marrone Foundation Publishing
1 Ridgewood Lane
Searcy AR 72143

*A special thanks to Nitzy, who challenged me
to talk about religion and politics.*

BOOK ONE

HOPE

I

"MMM, hmm. An elephant does live a long time, as they say; but a tortoise lives longer!"

Thomas was the oldest, wrinkliest, most crusty thing little Hope had ever seen. When he spoke, the words seemed to plod methodically one after another out of his mouth as slowly and ponderously as his feet did whenever he took a mind to walk somewhere, not that he took such a mind very often. Thomas was a Galapagos Island Tortoise, and he was speaking with Hope, a school-aged elephant.

"That's probably why my parents sent me to ask you about the origins of the Gardens instead of telling me themselves, Grandpa Tom."

"Mmm, hmm; yes, yes, so they did. But a tortoise doesn't live such a long time by being foolish! Hmm, hmm!"

"Grandpa Tom, I don't understand: what could be foolish about answering my questions—"

"Hmm. Yes, must be cautious. Mustn't be hasty. Think things through, as they say ..."

"Grandpa Tom," Hope tried to hide her blushing smile behind her plump trunk and peeked at him from behind her ear:

"No offense, but I don't think anyone would EVER accuse you of being hasty! Now come on: I'll gather up some of your favorite treats while you think about your answer. What can it hurt? You always say I need to focus on my school work, and this is for my history assignment."

Hope began to gather chunks of melon and juicy fruits from containers all around the area, then she piled them in front of the cantankerous tortoise. The whole time she did this, Thomas sat with eyes closed, occasionally emitting a grunt or hum, or clearing his raspy throat, but doing nothing to keep a casual observer from suspecting that he had drifted off to sleep, a state from which he never seemed distant.

Little Hope, having spent many of her afternoons with Thomas after school let out, was not to be fooled so easily. A number of times she had seen him feign sleep to avoid things for which he didn't care to exert himself. Hope was as patient as Thomas was stubborn. When one of his eyes cracked half a squint open to see if she'd left, Hope only smiled.

"HOW did the Gardens come to be, you say ... mmm hmm. Well, young lady, the things you're asking about happened a long, long, time ago, to be sure. Long before your teacher—that rascal Slylock—was a kit, mmm hmm. Long before old Greystone the African Grey was an egg. Even long before either of your parents were around—and they've been around a long time, to be sure."

As if his speaking style was not slow enough already, Thomas paused further to select a plump strawberry, which he chewed as cautiously as someone would chew a strawberry they feared might contain thorns or broken glass.

"Mmm, yes. Way back then things were, as you say, very different, to be sure. Animals everywhere were ruled by powerful kings. The lion and his cronies ruled with an iron paw, mmm, yes. They never lifted so much as a pinky claw to ease the burden of other animals, to be sure. All they did was lie in the sun, sleep all day, and devour everything meaningful that the other animals produced; they took so many young, mmm hmm, that it seemed at times whole families of animals might not survive, to be sure. Other animals couldn't hope to enjoy a peaceful old age, as the kings and their merciless henchmen preyed on the old and infirm as well.

"These kings of the Old Country never had the slightest concern for anyone but themselves and their own voracious appetites, to be sure. They marked territory, they fought to expand it, they preened, and they pampered themselves; all of their self-centered behavior, mmm hmm, at the expense of their poor, over-burdened subjects.

"These tyrants were never placed in authority because of ability or merit; they came to power through the most incompetent, inbred, nepotistic means possible: simple blood relation to previous, hmm, rulers.

"Part of what kept these Old Country rulers in power, to be sure, was their baboon witch doctors. They developed a cult that worked hand-in-hand with the lion kings to oppress the other animals. They used mumbly-jumbly nonsense words and mysterious rites to control the minds of most animals, and used persecution to manipulate the rest. They controlled the flow of information. By denying easily observable facts, they kept the animals from realizing the severity of their situation or recognizing the true cause.

"Some of the, shall we say, more militant animals tried to ease the burden of the masses of oppressed animals, to be sure, and change the status quo with insurrections and rebellions, all of which were suppressed with such ruthless cruelty that more moderate animals feared taking any action to improve their lot.

"However, to be sure, everyone has a breaking point. The need for a solution grew in proportion to the unreasonable actions of the, hmm, ruling families; and as that need grew, the freest thinking and most clever of the animals began to seek solutions.

"The solution that the world is most familiar with is this very community where you live, as they say: The Animal Zoological Gardens of Eden."

III

ALTHOUGH he had gotten — and kept—himself going for quite some time, Thomas' delivery still seemed perilously close to stalling and digressing into a nap at any moment. Sometimes as he blinked while speaking, his eyes looked loathe to reopen. Finally, chewing a chunk of fresh cantaloupe, Thomas resumed his tale with orange drool streamers dangling from each corner of his mouth...

"The Animal Zoo began as an attempt to solve many of these problems the animals faced, mmm hmm. Animals came from everywhere to live where, to be sure, they could rise above oppression by the few. Here, you see, they could have a voice in how they would get along, a say in who would govern, and a choice in how to worship; they would have the freedom to think, to speak, and as your name suggests, to hope. They came to LIVE. Hmm, yes, to be sure."

"I've never seen you so excited about anything, Grandpa Tom," Hope grinned, as only her deep familiarity with Thomas lent her the ability to see excitement in his lethargic discourse. "You must really think our history is something special!"

"Oh, it is little lady, to be sure. For the first time animals were to be equals, mmm hmm! They started from the idea, to be sure, that as far as the Keeper was concerned, they were equal, as they say. So, they built everything on that foundation: the system of leaders, and of picking leaders, to be sure, the system of rules and justice ... for once it didn't matter if you were a lion or a lamb, big or small, fast or slow, hairy or scaly, or feathered or bald, rich or poor, intelligent, or shall we say, less intelligent. Our Garden's beginning, to be sure, was the most glorious time in animal history."

"Was, Grandpa Tom?"

"Mmm hmm, yes … " Thomas' rheumy old eyes took on a faraway look, one of sadness and a deep weariness rather than the usual playful antics of an elder. "Hmm, hmm, yes … I'm a little tired, Pumpkin. Maybe we should, as they say, save your other questions for another, hmm, day."

IV

ON her way home, Hope thought about her talk with Thomas and how she would use it for her class assignment. As she walked alongside a thick hedge on her way, she suddenly smelled something so revolting it made her wrinkle her entire trunk in disgust.

"Ugh! Come out, Caspar, you stinky gas bag!" She half wheezed through choking spasms.

"How did you know it was me?" a pouting young warthog asked as he wriggled his ample, squat body through a thin spot in the hedge.

"How do you think? You smell like old socks and spoiled milk! Ugh!"

Caspar was unanimously regarded as the single most flatulent animal in the entire zoo complex, which was no mean feat. Somehow the mixture of his vociferous appetite, his lack of employing culinary quality control, and the heinous machinations of his gastrointestinal tract combined to produce the most frightening sounds and horrific odors imaginable. To the animals' sensitive sense of smell, his flatulence was an explosion of over-stimulation that left them in a state of olfactory shell shock.

"What—gasp—are you doing hiding around in hedges, anyway?"

"It's collection time for warthogs. I always try to stay away from home at collection time." Caspar watched his own feet kick listlessly at the dust, "My mom's always so sad that all she does is cry, and dad seems so far away—like he doesn't want to be close to us at all."

Assuming some of her friend's melancholy, Hope was quiet for a few moments, lost in her thoughts. Finally, she broke the silence and asked, "Caspar, what do you think collection time is? My parents act the same way, but they never want to talk about it."

"Well, of course I know what collection time is." He brushed his foreleg against his snout and sniffed, "only tiddy babies don't know THAT! I'm not a baby, but you must be! Hope's just a tiddy baby! Hope's just a tiddy baby!" he teased.

"Am not! Am not!"

The taunting and denials continued as the two proceeded along the hedge poking and jabbing each other. They both turned, however, when they heard someone approaching them and laughing.

"Ha, ha, ha! Yuk, yuk, yuk!"

"Oh, it's only you, Risa. I was afraid someone was laughing at us." Hope said.

"Hee, hee, hee! I am laughing at you!"

"Yeah, but hyenas don't count: you can't help it." Caspar added.

"What are you two arguing about, anyway? Heh, heh, heh."

Caspar ribbed, "the little baby here doesn't know what collection time is!"

Hope stamped her foot, "If you're so smart, YOU tell me!"

"If you don't know, I better not tell you. Uh, I might get in trouble or something."

"Humph!" smirked Hope. "Do YOU know, Risa?"

"Uh, ... uh, huh, huh, ... yeah. Why don't YOU tell her, Caspar?"

V

"WELL, okay," Caspar reluctantly began, "but don't tell ANYONE you heard this from me. If my folks found out that I was talking about stuff like this they'd kill me."

Hope and Risa exchanged a look that said both thought he was exaggerating a little too dramatically.

"Anyway, one time an older kid told me all about collection time, so I know it's true. Plus, he said if I could prove it wasn't true, he'd sniff one of my deadliest farts, so this is the real deal."

Caspar swelled his chest, building the expectation of the other two animals like a natural storyteller. "At collection time, a humongous vampire comes from a gigantic, dark castle far away. He flies on gross, slimy bat wings all the way here. He comes and bites adult animals in the neck. It's awful and it's very painful because he has huge, hollow fangs to suck their blood. Every so often, he gets hungry again and comes back to suck different animals' blood."

Caspar rose up on his haunches, which gave him enough height to almost look down at his two friends as he assumed a knowing air, "The vampire can only suck so much and then they have to have time to recover. If he fed on 'em again too soon, they'd have no blood left and they'd die and turn into zombies! That's why collection time is different for every different kind of animal: so he always has enough to eat but doesn't kill his source of food.

"And that's how come our parents are so upset during collection time. They've got no energy or patience left because they've been getting their blood sucked out by an evil vampire!"

"WHAT? Caspar, of all the crazy, dumb stories you've ever told, this is the WORST!" Hope's words were strong, but her eyes showed a hint of fear that there might be a nugget of truth in what Caspar had said. Mostly that fear stemmed from her complete lack of better answers.

Risa seemed even less impressed with Caspar's explanation than Hope. "Ha, ha, ha! Yeah, well, that's not what I heard. Har, har, har. And it was a big kid who told me, too—probably older than the one you heard your story from. So what really happens, heh, heh, heh, is that the food changes every so often. It takes the adults a while to get used to the new food, and that's why they're grumpier and moodier than usual. They all have trouble pooping and peeing anyway—it's always too often or not often enough, too much or too little, some funny color or smell, and they're off to the infirmary to get checked; change what they're eating, he, he, he, and it gets even worse! Hoo, hoo, hoo!"

"Now I KNOW you two are pulling my leg." Hope had lost almost all of the fearful look that her face had worn after the vampire story. "First of all, there's no such thing as vampires, so Caspar, you should focus more on your irritating bowel than your nonsense explanations.

"And Risa, your explanation doesn't have anything to do with collection time. Plus, OUR food doesn't even change like that. In fact, now that I think about it, the various hays and vegetables we eat are always the same, all year long. So are Grandpa Tom's fruits and melons.

"I should have known better than to believe you two clowns! You don't know anything about collection time and you don't have the guts to admit it!" She stamped her foot. "You just wanted to make me feel bad because I didn't know!"

The good feeling Hope had from discovering she wasn't behind her friends in finding things out almost entirely distracted her from the somewhat anxious feeling that collection time and her parents' reaction to it were very important. This unknown was like the dark space under a bed, or in a corner of a poorly lit room: scary because of what could be lurking there.

VI

NOT more than a couple of weeks passed before little Hope came home one day to find her mother rocking. When her mother was anxious—and especially at collection time—she would rock back and forth, her mighty trunk swaying just a half beat behind her body motion. Hope noticed a distance in her mother's eyes, and thought she looked too thin. Her little heart was bursting with sadness to see her mother this way.

As a much younger little elephant, she had not understood that this was an inappropriate time for her favorite line of questioning: when would she get a little brother or sister. At most times, her mother could field those questions with a sigh and a smile, and encouragement to keep hoping. She was able to counter Hope's persistence that it wasn't fair how her friends Risa and Caspar had brothers and sisters. It didn't work to explain to her how unique and special she was. But during collection time, her questions had gone unanswered entirely.

As Hope had matured, she had begun to notice the huge, salty tears eroding vast, cavernous wrinkles of infinite pain down her mother's face. Though she couldn't understand fully what was happening, she sensed that her questions added to her beloved mother's discomfort, so she held them in.

Now, when she saw her mother behaving in this way, she would spray fresh water on her back to cool her, and wave a branch over her to scare the biting flies away.

13

Hope's father was walking in circles around the habitat. He was only nominally less distant than her mother during collection time, once or twice answering Hope's inquiries by allowing that she would learn about it all too soon, or stating that once she knew, she'd wish she didn't.

And so Hope formulated a plan of action to unlock this mystery. She would take the thing that she wished to know, and bring it to the place of learning. She would ask her teacher.

VII

HOPE fidgeted expectantly as the other students took their places, being far more eager than usual for the old grey fox that taught their classes to arrive. Once he did, he was surprised how quickly her trunk shot into the air.

"Yes, Hope, do you have a question?"

"I do, Mr. Slylock: can you explain collection time, and why it causes our parents to act so strangely?"

Slylock had a habit of darting his beady black eyes back and forth over his students for feedback regarding how they were receiving what he was saying, a trait the students did not notice as they were mesmerized by his stately old body's dignified pacing and the slightly hypnotic swishing of his bushy tail. At hearing Hope's question, only the most astute observer would have noticed the shock and increased movement in his eyes. While he sighed and formulated his reply, Hope leaned forward in anxious anticipation, feeling she was on the very verge of learning something big, and that the something big was somehow shrouded in the mystery of the taboo.

Seeing her excitement and hoping to divert the class' attention, Slylock downplayed the collections. "Well, Hope, that is an unusual question—and not nearly as insightful as yours usually are. It is very simple and not overly important: you see, all the animals need to support our leaders so that our leaders can provide the things we need, like food, shelter, and protection. They even provide this school, Hope, so you can be sure to learn everything they have decided is important for you to know. Some animals get a little upset to do this because they are overly focused on their own losses rather than enjoying the gains our whole society receives as a result."

Slylock's eyes ferreted their way around the group happily noting that most students were too busy whispering or scratching themselves to listen at all; those who were listening had completely bought his empty diversion of an answer to Hope's question.

"But Mr. Slylock, what do you mean by support? I think all our parents are happy to help others all the time; what is it about this 'support' that is different during collections?"

With only the greatest effort the old fox managed to conceal his irritation that his first vague attempt did not satisfy Hope's curiosity sufficiently to avoid further questions.

"You know—we've studied this of course—that leaders throughout history have had to collect support in various forms in order to fuel the machinery of change and growth." Slylock permitted himself a small contented grin at his collection of idealisms strung together. He felt particularly quotable.

Hope interrupted his self-important revelry, "But Mr. Slylock, you still haven't said what you really mean by 'support.' What are you saying animals don't want to give?"

Faith the giraffe, with Charity the koala in her usual place wrapped tightly around Faith's neck, was beginning to give nonverbal signals of joining Hope's line of questions. Slylock, therefore, used the growing chaos in the rest of the classroom to disengage himself from the onslaught.

"Alright, alright! It's time to settle down over there. Hope, we'll have to back-burner our discussion and get on with our lessons because we're running behind. Who can tell me what we talked about yesterday?" Slylock's knowing eyes told him that Hope was unsatisfied with his vague answers, and not engaged in the current discussion; however, he at least had control of the class again. Maybe she would forget her question; maybe he would think of a better explanation. Anything to keep from having to tell them too much truth. "After all," he mused, "they're only children. There are things they shouldn't know."

BOOK TWO
SLYLOCK

VIII

HOPE often walked to school with her friend Faith, which provided her with a number of benefits. Of course, walking and talking with a friend was pleasant, but also Faith's long neck gave her an elevated position from which she could see Caspar from afar and issue an advance warning to prepare for the worst.

"Can you imagine how awful it must have been in the Old Country," Hope asked up toward her friend. "I mean, all those pompous lion kings with their heavy taxation, and taking all the young away to go fight over things that didn't matter to anyone but the lions anyway!" Hope's brow furrowed down, scrunching her eyes as she spoke—the closest to an angry look that the pudgy little pachyderm could achieve.

"And they wouldn't listen to anything the other animals said," added the lanky giraffe gliding on even, smooth strides beside her. "It must have been terrible to not have a say in anything! Not being able to vote or anything!"

"We can't vote NOW, silly!"

"But you know what I mean: Old Sly said even grownup animals in the Old Country couldn't vote—there were no selections to vote in." Faith's chin raised as she struck a dignified pose. "I can't wait to vote in the selections; I'm pretty grown up now, don't you think?"

"We're almost exactly the same age!" Hope huffed, tired of her friend always using her physical height as a measure of any good quality the two were discussing. "But you're right.

I can't even imagine a place with no vote, no selections, no say in ANYTHING! At least we can pick whichever leaders we like."

"And if we want, we could even try to get selected as leaders ourselves! ANYbody can be a leader if enough animals vote for them. I might just decide to be a leader one day," Faith goaded her friend, "others look up to me!"

"Very funny, stilts! I think your head's in the clouds." Hope turned to present herself in profile and extended her trunk, "But using your logic, I should try to get selected as a leader, too: I could BLOW AWAY the competition!" Hope accented her claim with a toot through her short trunk.

"If I get selected, I'd pick you as one of my helpers if you wanted. We could do all kinds of good things: we'd give speeches, we'd make good rules, we'd guarantee more good things for every animal, and it would be fun and games for everyone!"

"Well, I think I should be a leader and you could be my helper! I'd fix collection time so our parents wouldn't be so sad."

"Doesn't it make you wonder, though," Faith's tone turned more serious, "if the animals vote to select the best candidates in each selection, why aren't they doing these things already? Why don't they do something—ANYthing—to make things better?"

"Or," Hope added, "if they won't, why don't the animals select someone who will? That's a really good question, Faith. Remember what Ol' Sly says, though, 'We just have to believe; they're working together to make things better. But these things take time.' Who knows? Maybe it's for animals our age to fix!"

IX

HOPE and Faith turned their attention back to the path leading to school. They walked quietly for a couple of minutes, taking turns at kicking a piece of gravel ahead of themselves along their way.

"I'm almost big enough to see over the outer fence now."

"Yeah? Can you see anything out there yet?"

"Not really. But last night I did overhear my parents talking about something they saw. I guess some of the weaks ran over a squirrel again. Everything's so chaotic out there."

Animals in the gardens referred to a certain type of animal as "weaks," because their skin was so weak they had to cover it, their teeth were short and dull, they had no claws, some put things on their faces to help their weak eyes, and try as they might, no other animal had found a way to get them to understand the simplest communication, so they must have been weak-minded as well. They were too weak to walk or run very far, and rode around in boxes the zoo animals called weak-mobiles.

Outside the zoological gardens the weaks roamed in vast herds, and sometimes a few seemed to lose their bearings and wound up wandering around inside the zoo. They rarely caused problems inside, simply waddling around stupidly, pointing and making gibberish noises. Some animals, particularly the primates, were fond of making faces at them to see if the weaks would make faces back, for even in their mind-less stupidity they seemed capable of that.

"How do the weaks survive, I wonder? They seem to not be able to even find water or food; someone has to give it to them in bottles or bags," Hope said.

"Well, why do you think any other animal would choose to live out there with them? They're so dangerous in those weak-mobiles!" Faith shuddered all the way up her lengthy neck.

"Sounds AW-ful. I don't know if I'd even want to be tall enough to look out there and see all that: herds of weaks, zipping weak-mobiles, buildings instead of trees, crazy squir-rels and birds darting among the weak-mobiles and getting squished. Ugh! Terrible!"

"At least for dumb animals like weaks, their weaklings don't have to sit in school and listen to Ol' Sly droning on all day!" Faith joked.

"Speaking of which, here we are!"

X

"THE Great Experiment," began the old grey fox, as he paced slowly back and forth before his pupils, while his handsome tail flowed in such a stately manner as to command respect and admiration. "As we spoke about last time we were together," Slylock fairly oozed great learning, "the Animal Zoological Gardens of Eden—what we refer to today in short as the Animal Zoo—was seen by the intellectuals in the Old Country as an experiment, and by most of them as an exercise in futility, doomed to an inglorious end. Few believed that such a motley crew could successfully rule themselves without the authority of a lion king, or protect their community without his power, or grow as a civilization without his benevolent support of education and arts."

Slylock continued his methodical pacing, counting the points of his lesson off with a practiced paw. "These naysayers in the Old Country argued that regular animals were ill-equipped, either through stupidity or lack of noble blood, to rule themselves. Others saw the new Animal Zoo with a patronizing eye," Slylock mimicked to the best of his ability a patronizing aspect, "much like parents while watching their young playing at lion king games: content to allow the Animal Zoo to rule itself, but waiting expectantly to collect the spoils when it failed through mismanagement and infighting."

Slylock was on a roll, reciting the lesson nearly word-for-word as he had for years. "One of the first major hurdles to be crossed by the fledgling society was the 'Zooist Question,' involving whether the Gardens would be organized as one strong unit, or a loose federation of semi-independent habitats. The end result was something of a compromise: the individual groups of habitats—the reptile house, the bird house, the primate area, etc.—would enjoy some powers and local controls, while these smaller groups would form a great conglomerate with overall leaders—"

"But Mr. Slylock," the squirming Hope could contain herself no longer, "don't all these extra levels of leaders only result in the need for more and more of the 'support' you spoke of, 'support' that gets taken from the rest of the animals? If we select the best leaders, and they pick the best helpers, can't they do what needs to be done without all these extra leaders that take more "support"? Doesn't all this 'support' boil down to more collections that bring more unhappiness to the animals?"

Slylock's beady eyes ricocheted around the class like a couple of hundred grasshoppers on a hot sidewalk, while his mind raced to come up with another diversionary answer to this pesky little elephant's questioning. Meanwhile, his calm pacing and gently swishing tail distracted the students and pacified them.

"Of course," he practically purred like the fluffy cat he quite resembled, "it might seem so to you, but if you were as learned as I, you would see the perfect balance. Our system has to be this way, you see, because even the leaders participate in the collections. If they didn't, you'd have heard about it, right? So, surely you must understand that they would never do anything to make the collections more than they need be. They do everything possible to ensure each collection is absolutely necessary, and that each one is used in the most optimal way. Think about it this way, wouldn't the animals just select a different group of leaders if it weren't so?"

Old Sly's darting eyes evaluated the atmosphere in the entire class. Then suddenly he changed the direction in his pacing to visually sever the students' attention from Hope's question and thinking for themselves. Immediately he refocused their attention on the mind-minutiae of the zoological garden's early years.

"I still think you're crazy. One of these days you're going to get into trouble doing that," Faith warned Hope, both careful to walk upwind from Caspar, who waddled along contently behind them grunting and emitting noxious fumes.

"What are you talking about, Faith? This isn't the Old Country! Can't I ask a simple question? We just learned that was one of the patriarchs' big rules, right? Freedom to speak?"

BBRRAAAAAAACCCKKKKK!!

"CASPAR!" Hope and Faith exclaimed in unison.

"What? Don't I have freedom to speak, too?"

"Yeah, but your BUTT doesn't! That's disgusting!" Faith said through clenched teeth, straining her neck in an attempt to stretch up above any ill-wind.

"For your information," Caspar said haughtily, "it smells of rose petals and happiness."

"No it doesthn't. It sthmells of rotten eggsth and sthtink-weed," Hope lisped through her pinched-shut trunk.

"More like stagnant mud and dead fish," Faith interjected.

"Anyways," Caspar said, "whatever you think, it's my freedom to speak."

"That's not speaking, it's farting! The geese have more control of themselves than you do!"

"It's communicating, and Ol' Sly said that's what the patriarchs meant anyway."

"Whatever. You're still disgusting. You smell like a crusty old patriarch with foot fungus."

Faith returned to her original line of thought, bending over Hope, whose lips and trunk were still tightly closed with cheeks puffed out, a largely symbolic gesture of holding her breath as the argument with Caspar wound down.

"Still, Hope, you've gotta be more careful about what you say. You know you can get in trouble talking like that."

"How can I get in trouble? Isn't that what 'freedom to speak' is all about?"

"Now you're just being obnoxious, Hope." Faith said, "You know 'freedom to speak' doesn't mean freedom to say what you want, what you're thinking—"

"It means freedom to say what everyone wants to hear, or freedom to keep your mouth shut!"

"Thank you, Caspar, but I've got this. Pretty ironic coming from you, though. Anyway, you know you can't criticize the leaders, or teachers; you can't say anything that might offend another animal; you can't comment on any animal's color or ideas or age; you can't even mention the Keeper publicly; and you can't think of speaking about the legbits—"

"Shhh! They'll hear you!" cut in Caspar, thankfully with a non-malodorous communiqué.

As he spoke, the three friends glanced toward the flamingo lagoon, which they were passing at the moment. There were dozens of beautiful pink flamingoes with black and light-pink bills and yellow-ringed eyes. They were standing elegantly balanced on single legs in their shallow lagoon. Along with the flamingoes were three other creatures: a giraffe wearing black lipstick and yellow eye-liner wobbling precariously on one leg with the other three tucked away, an orangutan wearing the same cosmetics along with a flowered pink leotard, and a hippo that seemed to have been crudely painted pink with a large paintbrush alternately lifting one leg or another in a desperate attempt to appear to be balancing on less than all four.

Those pretending to be flamingoes were unofficially called 'legbits' because in trying to balance on one leg like flamingoes, since it wasn't natural for them, they looked like an animal that had suffered a bite or injury and had lifted the affected limb.

The three friends did not resume their conversation until they believed they'd passed out of earshot of the lagoon.

"CASPAR," Hope began as the three stared blankly back toward the flamingo lagoon.

"Uh, yes?"

"Did you, maybe, let a little something go? Something that might waft across the olfactories like a frightened stinkbug and rotten bleu cheese?"

Caspar ignored the question, entranced, while Faith sealed her nose and lips and puffed out her cheeks: a breath-holding preventative measure in the event that Caspar's flatulence opted to float up as high as her head.

"That is soooooooo weird," Hope said slowly.

"You can't say that!" hissed Faith, exhaling the words in a rush. "They really believe they're flamingoes. We have to respect that. Ol' Sly said so!"

"Now you sound just like him. Look, they aren't flamingoes. They weren't hatched as flamingoes. They can dress like them and try to imitate them, but that doesn't make them flamingoes."

Faith hooked her long neck to turn and look at her friend. "But doesn't Ol' Sly make sense? Aren't our thoughts more important than outside things like feathers and fur?"

Hope huffed, "Okay, smarty: if I really felt like I was a giraffe like you, would that make me a giraffe?"

"Don't be silly—that's different!"

"Okay," Hope tried a new tack, "what if Caspar here really thought he was Grandpa Tom, and sat still sleeping and munching melon chunks all day—and quit farting!"

"Apples and oranges."

"What if he thought he was Ol' Sly himself," Hope waved her trunk dramatically, "and paced and swished his little stub tail—"

"Hey! I happen to have a very nice tail!"

"—droning on about history? And telling us we have to pretend all those other animals are flamingoes when we can easily see they aren't?"

"Not remotely the same. He doesn't have a shell, so he can't be a tortoise, and he doesn't have long, silky fur, so he couldn't possibly be Mr. Slylock." Faith responded.

"But don't you see?" Hope jabbed her trunk repeatedly in the direction of the lagoon. "The legbits don't have feathers, they don't have bills, they don't have wings, they didn't hatch from eggs, their parents weren't flamingoes—do I have to go on? They aren't flamingoes no matter what they THINK they are!" Now she turned and poked her trunk at Faith. "How come if an animal thinks she's a poached egg, or even a weak, she's whisked away to the infirmary; but, the minute an animal that isn't a flamingo says he thinks he's a flamingo, the whole zoo bends over backwards to help him maintain his delusion?"

As the trio walked along, Hope's voice had risen until both Caspar and Faith had moved away slightly, and looked at her in fearful astonishment.

"I just feel sorry for them," cooed words as soft as the furry little ball that voiced them. The voice came from Charity's favorite tree, which the other three were just passing by. Looking up, they saw her almost lovingly hugging the trunk, until Faith moved close enough for her to cling to her neck instead.

"Isn't it sad that someone can be so lost and confused, and not have a single animal with enough love and courage to help them find their true identity? Instead they make them even more lost and confused."

Faith's head tilted in confusion at that remark. "Are you talking about those other animals who suspect that they might be flamingoes?"

"Oh, no. I'm talking about the ones who already think that they are."

XIII

SLYLOCK was as menacing as a thunderous, black, summer storm cloud, his pacing sharp, and his beady eyes aflame when the students arrived for class. His irritation rose another notch when he realized that his pupils were not going to notice that it was time to begin and automatically grow quiet out of respect for him. Instead, he would be forced to call them to order from the natural chaos to which they were so prone.

"Some of you had a busy day yesterday or so I hear," he said louder than his teaching voice to call them to order. He used the growing silence that followed to glare over the students, three in particular of whom squirmed guiltily and tried to glance innocently around like the others, wondering what Slylock was talking about.

"Yes, some of you think it is okay in our modern time, in our progressive, civilized society to meddle in other animals' business and make fun of those who are different, or those they don't understand."

Any chance that Slylock could have been talking about other little animals was quickly slipping away into the dark abyss of unknown trouble. The three little friends' vivid imaginations tortured them with potential punishments that their inquisitor Slylock might devise and inflict.

"Some in this very class choose to act like brute beasts—like weaks—and treat animals somehow unlike themselves with intolerance, subjecting them to persecutions and anxieties."

Slylock, turning from his pacing to glare in their direction, asked, "Hope, Caspar, Faith: do any of you happen to know anything about this? Does any one of you know someone who might be guilty of intolerance and tormenting animals with flamingo identities?"

"Do you mean the LEGBITS? Ha, ha, ha!" blurted Risa from the other side of the class.

Slylock spun on him like a serpent and struck, "WE DO NOT USE DEROGATORY TERMS IN THIS CLASS! They are animals with flamingo identities!" He added a more subdued rebuke for Risa's laughter, because he couldn't tell for sure if it was derisive or the characteristic manner of hyenas' speech.

"Mr. Slylock," came Charity's soft voice during the quiet moment before it seemed he might resume his attack on the little elephant, warthog, and giraffe. "Isn't the key trait you want us to learn acceptance of others' feelings even if different from our own? Aren't you trying to make us be tolerant of others' right to hold opinions which we don't share or agree with?"

"Why, yes! Yes, Charity, very good! Very good! Someone must be paying attention—"

"But I wasn't finished, Mr. Slylock," interjected Charity.

He smiled and gestured for Charity to continue, expecting her to essentially give the lesson for him.

"Doesn't that mean it's just as important to accept and tolerate the rights that Hope, Caspar, Faith, and Risa have? Isn't their right to their opinion as important as yours, or our leaders', or even the animals with flamingo identities?"

"NO!" The perfect situation Slylock had envisioned had imploded. The class was falling apart quicker than he ever could have foreseen, and he had no pre-formulated answers. He settled for, "That's different!" He saw rainbow colors and stars and huffed back and forth. "It's different for a number of reasons, reasons we are scheduled to cover in a later lesson." He hoped using his customary stalling techniques would save him again. "We don't have time to cover them all right now. We do need to break for lunch, and when we come back, we must get on with today's lesson!"

XIV

"BOY, that was close! I thought Ol' Sly was going to get us for sure!" Caspar's voice trembled as he eased his pressure by emitting a constant stream of sloppy-sounding gas.

"I for oned, wish you wud focus a liddle less ond being scared, and a liddle bore ond nod foobigading your ondly freds ind da world!" Hope admonished through her tightly pinched nose.

Faith craned her neck and even tilted her head far back in a futile attempt to find breathable air somewhere above the fear-stench cloud. "Caspar, you are impossible! You have not stopped farting once since we left class! If we could only harness your energy—"

"Hey, look! Over near the zebra paddock!" Charity had her usual high vantage point, clinging to Faith's long neck, but she could see farther ahead since, for whatever reason, she wasn't craning and tilting and teary-eyed like her tall friend.

When the other animals looked, they saw two zebra foals swirling around each other in a cloud of dust.

"Isn't that Lamont and Homer?"

"Looks like. Wonder what they're beefing about."

One of the antagonists suddenly reared and swung his hoof violently, just grazing the head of the other, who howled, ducking under the brunt of the blow to take an angry bite of his assailant's neck.

"Trashy OREO! Get your germ-infested teeth off me!" he screamed while he swung around and kicked with both hind hooves, catching his opponent in the side and sending him reeling backwards.

"Dirty SKIDMARK! You kick like a mare! Prob'ly 'cause your momma's a dirty skidmark just like you!"

This comment so infuriated the other foal that he roared through bared teeth while charging, such that the two foes hit shoulder-to-shoulder and wound up rolling in the dust, kicking and biting in a frenzy.

During the fight, the other animals had come running over, but it was only with the greatest effort that they were able to separate the two little zebras.

"Don't know why you pulled me off," Lamont panted. "I almost had that peckerwood skidmark."

"You didn't almost have nothing but an even fatter lip, you bubblegum oreo," Homer growled, chest heaving.

"What's this all about?" a newly arrived polar bear cub asked.

"Well, Forrest, that dumb, porch-donkey oreo insulted me. He oughta know he should talk more respectfully to his betters."

Lamont reared and struggled to get loose from Faith and Caspar. "You better watch what you say, dirty skidmark! You can't run, can't jump, can't neigh, can't play zebra games, nothing! You're just a no good, fly-bitten, honky, dirty-under-wear-looking, polebarn-trash SKIDMARK!"

Quite a crowd had gathered by this time. Hope and her friends had managed to gently move in between the combatants, and their taunts began to lose a little force as they tired and as the physical distance between them grew.

"Come on Bubba, come on Jade; let's leave these losers!"

Lamont shook himself free from Faith and Caspar and, joined by the alligator and panther he had just addressed, walked away from the crowd with a couple of chimps and a black bear.

Trying to assert an equal amount of independence and control, Homer shook himself loose from Hope and Charity, and, calling to some of his friends in the crowd, left in the opposite direction with an albino crocodile, a snow leopard, a pale orangutan, and the polar bear cub.

Hope and Charity found Faith and Caspar as the crowd thinned out.

"I'll never understand why those two are always at each other," Hope sighed. "I'd love to have another elephant my age to play with."

"Well, what's the matter with us?" Caspar asked, grinning, tusks akimbo.

"Don't get butt-hurt, Caspar. I mean, I'd like it if you didn't kill me with your stinky farts all the time, but you're good friends, all of you. It would just be nice sometimes to talk with someone a little more like me who could understand me better."

"Those two don't make it seem like it would necessarily work that way! Maybe you're better off," Caspar assumed a dignified air, "with an aromatically gifted friend like me!"

"Or, maybe you're better off simply because you're wiser than Homer and Lamont, and have a better way of thinking."

The other three animals looked up at Faith and could tell she was pondering something deep. They waited for her to continue.

XV

"I know how much you like a nice grassy spot under some tasty trees," Charity said, climbing back up Faith's neck. "There's one over there where you can sit down and tell us what you're thinking, while I climb up and get some of your favorite leaves for you."

Hope and Caspar skipped along with Faith's long, graceful strides to the place Charity had indicated, and after Faith had carefully folded her legs away and gotten comfortable with the others gathered around her, she began to speak.

She inclined her neck a little toward where Hope, like a roly poly, had curled up on her backside holding her hind legs with her front ones. "Who did you see walk away with Lamont?"

"Oh, I don't know; some of his friends I guess, like Jade and Bubba. I seem to remember seeing a black bear, so probably Smoke, and maybe the chimps."

"And did you see who went off with Homer?" Faith inquired.

"Well, Forrest, and um, Pinkeye and Snowball, but I don't know who else—"

"I know!" blurted Caspar. "I saw Yellow the orangutan, and I think I saw a couple of snow monkeys."

"Okay," continued Faith, "what do you notice about these groups?"

"Ha, ha, ha! A guessing game? Why didn't you guys invite me?" Risa asked, having arrived unnoticed. He plopped down with the others. "Hoo, hoo, hoo! I love guessing games!"

"It's not a guessing game! Be serious for one minute if you can. Faith just asked what we noticed about the groups that Lamont and Homer walked off with after their fight today." Hope explained.

"That's easy, har, har, har. Lamont walked away with dark-colored animals, and Homer left with light-colored ones."

"Don't be ridiculous, Risa," Hope scowled. "I just asked you to be serious!"

"Hope, Risa isn't as far off as you think. Go back over what you saw in your mind for a minute."

Hope scrunched her pudgy face deeper into the scowl and released her hind legs to fold her front legs over her chest defiantly. Hmph, she thought to herself, no way was it as simple and as silly as that!

But as the realization that what her friends were saying could be true began to sink in, her brow unfurrowed, her front legs uncrossed and returned to wrap around her hind ones, and a visible wave of resignation swept over her entire demeanor.

"But what about Homer and Lamont themselves?" she squeaked in a final defense, "They're both black AND white, right?"

"That's technically true, Hope, but one is proud to be black with only stripes of white, while the other is proud to be white with only stripes of black." Faith explained.

"Faith's right, Hope." Charity's words, as always, were accompanied with a reassuring hug. "We've all heard them argue that point many times."

"But they're both ZEBRAS! What does black on white or white on black even matter? They're so alike it's stupid!" Hope pleaded.

Charity was still hugging Hope's foreleg as her neck was

too thick for stubby koala arms. "Are any of the others less ridiculous, Hope? What's the difference between a jaguar and a snow leopard? Or an alligator and an albino crocodile? Or a black-colored bear and a white-colored bear?"

"Remember, Hope," Faith added gently, "that was one reason for the horrible zoo riots and fighting Mr. Slylock taught us about. The whole garden was almost destroyed when the animals fought over whether one animal could make another animal work, but also because of differences in color!" Faith placed a hoof softly on Hope's shoulder.

"But that was so long ago. Those hard feelings should be over. Aren't we all smart enough to see we're basically the same? That we're equal?"

Faith's hoof rubbed Hope's shoulder in soothing circles as she smiled. "And that's why I said you have a better way of thinking, Hope. It's very ignorant to imagine great differences between animals, when the only real difference is external: a slightly different color. But there are still plenty of animals—in both groups—that prefer to be ignorant rather than simply growing up and taking responsibility for themselves."

"Hee, hee, hee. Sounds like they're looking at the world through dork-colored glasses! Ha!"

"Any time you look at the world through any colored glasses, you aren't seeing the world as it truly is." Faith stood and stretched, and along with the rest of the young animals, said goodbyes to her friends, who began strolling toward their homes for the night. She called over her shoulder, "And if you can't even see the world as it truly is, you can't be right about anything can you?"

XVI

HOPE'S melancholy lifted during her short walk home, after the fashion of the young and indefatigable. When she arrived, she bounded into her mother's embrace. "I love you, Mama! Where's Papa?"

"Oh, Pumpkin! I love you, too! But let's allow your father to rest a bit. He's had a hard day."

"Doing what, Mama?"

"Well, the leaders are putting up a tent for some summer events, so he had to pull ropes to raise that, and drive stakes to tie the ropes to. He had to carry heavy materials to build a stage and many other tasks."

"But I thought animals weren't supposed to make other animals work anymore. Not after the riots. Wasn't that one of the rules after the riots, Mama?"

Her mother gently caressed Hope's head and ears with her trunk while Hope fidgeted and wriggled her stubby trunk all over her mother's.

"Hope, dear, you're such a clever child," she sighed. "Sometimes I don't know what we're going to do with you!"

"But Mama, you didn't answer my question at all! Papa shouldn't have to do all that because animals don't make other animals work anymore, right?"

Hope's mother smiled warmly and leaned her head at an incline. "Dear, Papa's not working for other animals. He simply does what has to be done for the gardens. That's how we get our food and shelter."

"But aren't animals telling him what has to be done?"

"I suppose, dear; I hadn't really thought about it. It isn't his plan or something he'd be doing anyway, so someone must tell him what needs doing." A slightly puzzled look flashed across the enormous mother's face, replaced by the usual peaceful one.

"Well, that sounds like one animal making another one work to me, even if it doesn't to anybody else. And Papa shouldn't have to do it! If the leaders need some tent for something, why don't they put it up themselves?"

"I suppose they're too busy leading to do it, Hope."

BOOK THREE

FAITH

XVII

WHEN Faith arrived home following the incident between the zebra foals, she and her parents greeted each other by intertwining necks and nuzzling. They majestically strolled together along the edge of a copse of trees, occasionally stripping some succulent leaves from the branches with their long, prehensile tongues.

Faith's father's coloring was nearly white between patches of light beige, while her mother was burnt orange under patches of very dark brown. The young giraffe mentioned to her parents that on her way home, she had seen a fight sparked by colorism.

"You know that your father and I don't think that way, Faith," her mother began, looking at her through enormous, dark eyes under lush, full lashes, "but tell me, how do you and your friends feel?"

"I'm so happy you and Dad talk with me about things I might see, hard things, like this. Most of my friends feel like we do, only they don't understand it as good because they don't learn about it at home."

"As well, dear. They don't understand it as well."

"Of course, Dad. As well. Anyway, it's hard for us to believe something as dumb as color meaning so much to anyone. I mean, can you imagine me loving one of you and not the other because you're different shades? How stupid!"

Faith's mother began to explain, "But Sweet-patches, before the riots—"

"And some animals even now, dear," cut in her father.

"—That's right, some animals still think like animals did before the riots. They would have taken issue with your dad and I being together, simply because we're different shades. They would even have treated you badly for being our child."

"Mom, do you think all the animals in the gardens will ever respect each other without worrying about color or whatever other silly thing they have that's different?"

"I don't know, dear. Remember what your father always says: you can't control anything past the reach of your own neck. As long as someone is so insecure that he tries to bolster his self-worth by focusing all his energy on being better than someone else, he'll keep looking for ways to compare and divide. It's only when you're confident of your own value that you can devote those energies to something more productive. Something like celebrating things we share, things that bring us together, and moving forward together."

"Dad, what do you think?" Faith asked, turning to the gentle giant striding at her other side.

"I think our society and the animals in it can change—and change for the better—so long as we believe in something better, and so long as we act on our belief." He swung his great neck over to playfully butt his head at his precious daughter. "That's why we named you Faith!"

XVIII

FAITH smiled as she walked along with her shorter, stockier friend. Hope beamed at the great white and orange striped tent. She nodded approvingly at the perfectly aligned stakes and ropes, and the way she strode may have left the viewer with the opinion that she had been the supervisory planner of the entire shebang.

Up and down every sidewalk leading to the tent, a myriad of exciting sideshows caught the little animals' eyes: street actors, contortionists, and acrobats. Snack vendors filled the air with alluring smells. As Faith and Hope walked along, other friends joined them.

"Look at that!" cried Hope, and her friends followed her trunk pointing to see Chester, the python, who had tied himself into a seemingly impossible knot.

Farther along, each took a turn providing a backdrop for Senator, the bug-eyed chameleon, who could change his appearance to match anything he chose. He demonstrated by blending in with Hope's grey back, Charity's white and grey fur and little black hands, and even Faith's pattern of brown patches on yellow. He matched Risa's tawny fur with black spots. From there he climbed onto Caspar's back.

"Well, I can't see him," Faith said, bending down over Caspar and squinting, "but I bet if we sniff, he'll be the only part back there that doesn't smell bad!"

"Hey!" Caspar objected.

"Look! They're starting! Let's go to the tent!"

Animals filed into the humongous tent from all approaches and arranged themselves around the centrally located stage. Then the leaders began to arrive and fill in the areas immediately around the stage and finally the stage itself. The animals recognized council members, department chiefs, cabinet members, representatives, magistrates, and finally the deputy lordmayor, the vice deputy lordmayor, the assistant lordmayor, and the lordmayor himself.

The leaders cleared their throats, strained their necks, and waved at real or imaginary friends among the animals throughout the tent. They leaned conspiratorially toward assistants or colleagues as if whispering vital information, and all wore very serious expressions on their faces to unmistakably convey the deep gravity of any communications with which they were entrusted—obviously directly proportional to their own vast importance to the governance and continued operation of the gardens. A few could be caught glancing at the light and shadows playing on the inside of the tent roof, a dead giveaway that they were trying to judge the time, eager to get the event started and over with as soon as possible.

The occasion was an opportunity for various leaders to give speeches, and for challengers to give responses so that the animals gathered could determine which candidates to vote for in upcoming selections. Several leaders, one after another, came to the front of the stage and made preliminary remarks.

Each claimed an intention to be brief, and then failed miserably.

Faith craned her neck and slowly panned across the group of leaders before her. Her brow began to cloud.

"Hope," she whispered. "Does anything stand out to you about the animals on and around the stage?"

"Um … they're the leaders?"

"Yes!" Faith hissed. "Of course that! Anything else?"

"Hmm … well, now that you mention it, they're almost all lions—"

"And the ones that aren't might as well be: couple of tigers, cheetahs, pumas—all meat-eating great cats!"

Hope asked, "Do you think there's a chance that it matters?"

Faith replied, "Do you think there's a chance that it doesn't?"

XIX

THE pre-selection speeches and debates were heated. No matter what question arose, two sides immediately formed. If one lion spoke on the need to increase rainfall in the gardens, his opponent would demonstrate how the zoo could only survive if rainfall decreased. If one proposed switching from alfalfa to clover hay for economic gain and improved diet, his counterpart would convincingly make the case for alfalfa being of superior nutritional value and cost effectiveness.

No matter which side addressed an issue, one thing was consistent: no speaker ever stated any of his plans concretely enough to make an evaluation of its potential effectiveness. If asked how exactly he intended to increase rainfall in the gardens, the lion responding might refer to his track record, or he might quote from his previous speeches. Another would gesture convincingly with his foreleg, or make big-eyed sad faces, showing hurt because his answer wasn't accepted at face value.

"I have experts evaluating the data right now, even as we speak," he might say. "And we're finding them very close to our initial forecasts. Once we get the green light we can begin to move forward—and this is the kind of change for the better I stand for!"

Most of the leaders and aspirants were aligned with one of two groups: the "Everybody Rules Party," and the "Yeah U Kans," or ERPs and YUKs respectively. Strangely, the two groups' ideologies were so fluid that the positions each group took during a particular selection were determined in large part by the first speaker to make a claim. For example, if a YUKer was the first during pre-election speeches to propose that the gardens' wilder animals such as squirrels and rats be treated as zoo animals, then that year at least you could be sure that the ERPers were of the opposite opinion, protesting that wilder animals were too dangerous and therefore should be treated as weaks or worse. In a subsequent selection, if an ERPer addressed the issue first, he might turn the tables and welcome the wilds, causing the YUKers to have to oppose them and their previous position.

As confusing as much of this was to the other animals, the candidates made things even more murky by resorting to personal attacks on their opponents when they ran out of quasi-legitimate issues to debate.

"My worthy opponent has a history of demeaning this august office by scratching himself in public," one might say in response to a legitimate claim by the other that he didn't have a hoot of experience in any leadership role.

"Anyone who has been close to the other candidate is aware he has the oral hygiene of a Komodo Dragon," another might state, when all relevant jabs had been expended.

After endless hours of speeches, posturings, accusations, and attacks and counterattacks, most of the animals were left without the slightest clue as to what had really transpired, least of all the leaders. For an understanding of what had really been said and what it meant, they did not listen to the speeches anyway. For understanding, they relied on the recaps provided by 'expert commentators.'

XX

"**T**HANK you, Phil, for that weather-guess. AWWK! Next up: our own leader-speech analyst, Greystoke, who was on the scene at today's selection speeches. Good evening, Greystoke, how are you?"

"Wonderful, Polly, thank you. You're absolutely right, we had some very interesting speeches today. And to discuss them with me, I'm pleased and honored to be joined by our good friend and colleague, the gilded macaw best known for his expert leader analysis, Winston. Winston, welcome!"

"Thank you, Greystoke. Hello, Polly. I'm so glad to be here."

A crowd was gathering at the foot of the imitation tree where the three birds were perched, one on each of three broomstick-looking fake branches sprouting at right angles to each other and the trunk. The animals inched forward, faintly breathing through open mouths, glassy-eyed, mesmerized by the conversation of the birds.

"AWWK! Do you know what struck me, Winston—"

"I don't, Polly."

"—was that not one of the leaders mentioned AWWK! crackers in all the time they were speaking."

The underlying hum consisting of animals creeping forward, breathing, and jostling one another occasionally increased in volume due to murmurs of assent or disagreement.

"Well, Polly, I did notice one thing, and I'm almost certain Greystoke keyed in on it as well."

"AWWK! What's that, Winston?"

"Greystoke? One chance to steal my thunder?"

"Go ahead, Winston. I'm eager to hear your take."

"Well, okay. We heard no speeches from lionesses today. What implications do you see from that?"

A careful observer would note that the murmurs, either of approval or disagreement, had little to do with what the birds said. Rather, some animals simply had agreeable dispositions and continually muttered assent. Other animals, from the well of their own disagreeable natures, continually muttered negatively. Neither group applied much thought to anything the analysts said; or even whether their analysis accurately reflected the speeches the animals had just heard for themselves.

"AWWK! What do you think that means for the rest of us in the gardens?"

"Good question, Polly," Winston began.

"First we have to determine whether there really is an issue there." Greystoke interjected.

"And that's right, Greystoke. The way we do that is simple mathematics. What's the ratio of lionesses to lions? Then we take that ratio and compare it with what we observed on stage today and see if there is a discrepancy. So why aren't there more lionesses up on that stage?"

"Well, we need to examine demographics, don't we? I mean, who's voting to select lionesses?"

"AWWK! The cubs!"

"Ha ha! Cute, Polly, but obviously they're too young to vote—"

"And maybe that's why AWWK! no lionesses are selected as leaders!"

"So, Polly brings up a good point, Winston. Is it time to let young cubs vote? And if cubs vote, what about other young animals?"

"Well, Greystoke, lots of possibilities there. There's the young vote that you mentioned, there's the problem of setting a ratio that we can live with and forcing our choices to meet that ratio, then there's altering our leadership structure to add a lioness council to augment the lion council—"

"AWWK! AWWK! AWWK! It's so complicated, Winston!"

"Well, Polly, that's leadership!"

XXI

AT the same time that Polly, Winston, and Greystoke were analyzing the leaders' speeches at the imitation tree outside the great tent, near-identical scenes were being enacted at a dozen locations throughout the zoo. These were the bird shows.

Beside the snow cone kiosk, two penguins and a puffin critiqued the leaders on the positions regarding the effect of animal flatulence on the climate. They discussed voluntary versus mandatory emission controls, and whether controls in the Animal Zoo were pointless if the overwhelming majority of animals in the world remained unregulated. They presented hypothetical models showing the adverse effects of current emission levels on zoo habitats. The audience murmured its concern.

A little further from the big tent, near the entrance to the bird house, a cockatoo, a flamingo, and a lorikeet regaled before the gathered animals the fashion statements that various leaders had made or failed to make. They compared manes, grooming, and oral hygiene. They judged mannerisms, non-verbals, gestures, and all aspects of speaking style unrelated to content. The animals watching this bird show seemed to include many of the zoo's most vain, who constantly preened themselves during the presentation, glancing furtively around to see if anyone else was looking at them.

Around the corner from the bird house and down a bit toward the monkey menagerie, a noble eagle, a severe-looking falcon, and a harsh-colored fighting cock discussed how the speakers had approached the issue of claw control—the question of what rights animals had to claws, talons, and spurs. Although the right to claws had been clearly and perpetually guaranteed by the founders in the zoo's charter (mostly as a protection against future oppression), later leaders fearing violence between animals sought to limit those rights. They considered restricting which animals could have claws, how many they could have, and what length claws could be. Those particularly interested in the issue were present at this bird show: including bears, canines, felines, and raptors.

Near the combined infirmary/nursery complex, doctors Chip and Dale served as special medical consultants for a bird show hosted by a myna and a mockingbird. They analyzed the leader speeches on the topic of medical care. If the animals had not been confused by the leader speeches, they were sure to be boggled even more by this bird show. The mockingbird dragged every question or comment back to the issue of medical care for wilder animals—pulling quotes from everyone into his argument—while the doctors acted like typical chipmunks. They chased back and forth, interrupted one another, and alternated between overly complex medical jargon and oversimplified chattering. Still the audience murmured contentedly.

Interestingly, for each bird show covering a given topic of interest, an alternative bird show assured its audience of the opposite position: that flatulent emissions had nothing to do with the overall climate, that externals and fashion meant little in leaders, that claw controls save lives, for example.

Hope's mother and father passed these and other bird shows without a glance. They walked together, trunks entwined, their great bulks gently swaying in harmony. Just before they arrived home, however, their attention was diverted momentarily from one another to a small crowd gathered around a bird show consisting of a screech owl, a barn owl, and a cuckoo.

XXII

THE bird show Hope's parents paused in front of was already in progress.

" … and that's why the YUKers feel so strongly about this point, Vivian, SCREEE! We didn't have choices in the Old Country. Everybody just did what the king wanted, and HE wasn't even the result of animals' choice—"

"WHO! This isn't about choices, Locura, as the ERPers stated clearly, it's about whether it's right or wrong to kill defenseless young animals—"

"SCREEE! Come on, Vivian! You're blowing this way out of proportion with that charged language. After all, we're only talking about extra young that the parents don't want anyway. SCREEE! They'd likely starve if left alone."

The two grey mountains on the outskirts of the audience sighed deeply, their great drooping shoulders a picture of heavy sadness.

"That's not even remotely true, Locura, and you know it. As the ERP council-lion showed graphically, there are literally dozens of parents—WHO!—parents in this zoo with less young than they desire, while your irresponsible YUKer friends spew out young, only to decide they don't really want them. So they—WHO!—eat them!"

The gigantic, salty tears that burned a hot path down the wrinkles of Hope's mother's face might as well have filled her ears instead of her eyes. She heard nothing more of the analysis of the leader speeches. Her massive lungs sighed pitiably, as Hope's father led her the rest of the way home.

XXIII

THE following week, the young animals were abuzz before class with discussions about the leader speeches—or, more accurately about the bird show commentaries on the leader speeches. Old Slylock had told his class to attend the speeches and to be prepared to discuss them at their next class meeting.

Overachieving, teacher's-pet-type pupils assumed all-knowing, smug airs, while chatting about the speeches. They sighed and looked condescendingly at their peers, certain that the others couldn't possibly have comprehended the complexities of the speeches as well as they had.

On the opposite end of the spectrum were students likely of equal intelligence, who nonetheless failed to see attending either school or the leader speeches as important. These students stood on the fringes of the groups of their peers doing the same thing they did standing on the fringes during the speeches: mocking anyone who took the proceedings seriously. They mocked the wandering eye or the drooping ear. They made fun of bad teeth or ridiculous hair. They imitated voices, cruelly exaggerating any anomaly. Though pretending to ignore the speech contents, they also harshly criticized leaders who answered questions poorly or who avoided answering entirely. They pulled no punches when leaders gave nonsensical explanations, or patently absurd solutions. Focusing their energies in this manner, they saw the leader speeches and the entire selection process as fake and hypocritical.

Faith and her friends were both spatially and ideologically somewhere between these two extreme camps.

The conversation lagged momentarily after the overachieving crowd had smugly regurgitated every angle and unoriginal thought they had borrowed from the various bird shows. The pause was just long enough to move Faith to test an idea of her own, one that had never been breathed by the leaders, or whispered by the analysts.

"Isn't it strange how almost all the leaders are lions?" her soft, hesitant voice floated down to the other animals.

"That's what I was saying," broke in an overachiever who had listened to Greystoke, Winston, and Polly. "There really should be a greater number of lionesses—"

"No, no! You misunderstood me." Faith earned a scowling glare from a peer unaccustomed to being contradicted or interrupted. "I mean, isn't it strange how almost all the leaders are lions, as opposed to any other kind of animal. In fact, you found it odd that there were no lionesses, but what about hens or mares, or cows or does? What about females or males of any other kind of animals? Why just lions?"

"Don't be silly," began an egoistic young ostrich who struggled unsuccessfully to add to her condescending tone a downward glancing smirk at the young giraffe standing over her. "That's just who was selected—"

"But don't you see? The only choices for selection are lions! How can we select anyone but lions when they're all that even speak for selection?" Faith argued.

"I don't understand what your problem is. It's very simple," said a self-important sloth, hanging upside down, which gave him the illusion of looking down on the much-higher Faith. "Lion kings were bad in the Old Country. Here we are fortunate to be able to select our leaders. It's so much better. Everyone says so."

Slylock stole in quietly and listened, unseen at the back, while the young animals debated.

Faith held fast, unconvinced by her classmates' cookie-cutter answers. "Hmm. I just don't see a huge difference. Both in the Old Country and here the leaders are lions. The only difference is that name, 'king'—"

"No! Here we get to pick WHICH lion—"

"But it's always still a lion! What if there are some other animals that could do a better job? Or some that understand the rest of us better? Or some that we could trust more? What if our leaders chose assistants because of how smart or capable they were, instead of choosing their friends and whoever helped them get selected?" Faith's long neck swerved this way and that as her gaze shifted from one young peer to another. "What if there were animals who would lead and make the best decisions for the whole Animal Zoo instead of just for the animals who give them gifts? Wouldn't it be better if we could select these animals?"

Slylock cleared his throat noisily and called the class to order before officially starting the discussion of the leader speeches. "Faith, I'll give you a little credit for creativity, but your issue is not a very big one." His beady eyes darted around the class as he slowly paced and swished his tail hypnotically. "If it were important, of course the experts would have addressed it. The real reason that more animals aren't leaders is that they must not want to be, or must not be qualified. All it takes is speaking for selection, right? Why, we might very well have a future lordmayor or leader right here in this very class! Anyone want to be lordmayor of the Animal Zoo when you grow up?"

A dozen forelegs shot optimistically skyward.

"Of course, we have life so much better than our ancestors, who could never hope for such freedoms or opportunities under the harsh oppression of the lion kings. Here we can shoot for the stars! We can vote to select whichever leaders we believe will help us most. We aren't forced to live under a lion king!"

"No," Faith muttered to herself, "we get to pick which lion we're forced to live under ..."

BOOK FOUR
RISA

XXIV

FAR too early in the morning, the Animal Zoo residents were jarred awake by maniacal laughter. It echoed through the still-dewy mists of the peaceful pre-dawn calm, irreparably shattering the most peaceful time of the day.

All across the gardens animals awoke with a start and quickly checked the safety of those dear to them. As they came to the conclusion that the sound came from far away, many rolled their tired eyes this way and that, trying to pin-point the laughter's origin.

Several sleepy-eyed young animals believed they almost rec-ognized the laughter in the fog. One little elephant said what all the others were thinking: "That had better not be Risa!"

The same birds who had discussed the leader speeches were out in their usual places, but they were there long before their usual time. They were disheveled, red-eyed, and ruffled, but they were dishing out the scoop in various forms and formats across the zoo, snippets of which could be utilized to piece a partial story together.

" ... just can't understand how something like this could occur in our community, Gina. I mean, this is what we'd expect in uncivilized places," scowled a somber-looking bird, while casually adjusting the water dish and seed bell in front of him.

" ... and they aren't releasing the name of the victim at this time, Randy, awwwk," droned a parrot with her wing held to her ear.

" ... no suspect yet, Virgil," a goggle-eyed emu stated, "but we have been assured that the deputy chief lion for the Department of Public Safety will be making a statement later this morning."

" ... it seems one of our own young animals found the victim of this gruesome killing, which resulted in the shrieks many of our faithful listeners heard early this morning. As we would expect, he was pretty shaken up, Alexa ..."

" ... the entire area will be off limits until the authorities complete their investigation ..."

" ... classes will be cancelled today, but counselors will be available for any young animals who have difficulties coping with the events of this morning."

" ... that's really all we know right now, Bill, but as new information becomes available, we'll be sure to keep you updated all morning as this story unfolds ..."

XXV

BY midmorning, the number of birds chattering about what had occurred had skyrocketed. Birds filled all the imitation trees. Others lined the edges of building roofs. They filled the real trees between the animals' habitats.

Once they had exhausted all the known facts—which were few—their discourses began to drift farther from those facts and deeper into pure speculation.

"… Steve, would this tragedy have been averted if our leaders had enacted the more strict claw control rules they recently considered?"

"… Well, Lisa, those rules would have restricted each animal to not more than four claws per limb, none of which could be extended further than six inches from the cuticle; but even an animal in compliance with these restrictions could have still caused the injuries we imagine were involved in this situation."

"… Does this seem like the work of an individual, Dick, or are we seeing the result of clan violence again?"

"… Of course, Rita, everyone is concerned about these clans and what they're doing. We know that they give angry youths a place where they are accepted, where they have structure, and where they feel they have a chance to 'be somebody', even if that somebody is a violent, antisocial beast."

"… Ted, is there anything in all this that makes you suspicious—as many are—that the authorities are somehow behind this, either officially, or if not, then perhaps a scenario in which an off-duty lion might have gone rogue?"

"That's a very good question, Crystal, and one that we really need to consider. Do these authorities have too much power? Should somebody be watching to ensure that those charged with our safety aren't overreacting or even mistreating the animals they're supposed to be protecting? We need more facts in this case, but ..."

"...What about this young hyena who found the remains, Chris? I hear there are animals who criticize him because they feel a heinous killing like this is no laughing matter—his actions seem incredibly insensitive at least!"

"Too soon, Jackie?"

"That's what some are saying, Chris. But the Wild Dog Society has come out strongly in support of this young hyena, labelling him a hero. They say that's just the way he expresses himself, and if he hadn't raised such an alarm, who knows how long it might have been before the victim of this terrible tragedy was found."

"Good point, Jackie, good point."

"...Have the authorities come up with a motive yet, Albert? There must be some reason behind such an atrocity."

"...If they have, Susan, they aren't divulging it just yet, so we're still left to speculate at this time."

I
N the ensuing days the myriad birds reporting from their various perches continually rehashed the same mind-numbing information over and over. Occasionally, YUKers blamed ERPers, or ERPers assured listeners that YUKer policies led to the violence.

A few birds on the very outer fringes of the gardens expressed the opinion that pressure from over-collection and discontent over class differences may have contributed to the tragedy. The few animals watching these bird shows thought for themselves. As a result, they were viewed with suspicion by the other animals. Faith's family, if they watched bird shows at all, watched these.

Risa was often featured in the mainstream bird shows. At first, he drew crowds who gleaned something of the trauma of the event from his haggard looks and faraway stare. Hyenas are not the neatest, trimmest animals to begin with, but lack of sleep was wreaking havoc with his appearance.

Later, as he became more callous through repeating his story, he drew crowds eager to hear the gory details of the killing. Eventually exhausted by the attention, he began avoiding the bird shows as much as possible.

His friends, originally sympathetic, changed their attitude as well. They went from compassionate toward his fear and suffering, to jealous of his time in the limelight.

"Hee, hee, hee. There you guys are! I've been looking all over for you."

"You probably don't want to come over here, Risa."

"Heh, heh, heh, why? Is Caspar airing his thoughts again?"

"No, because there's no birdshow crowd to impress over here." Caspar turned to one side to imitate Risa speaking, "I think the victim's name was Olive, Mr. Birdshow Guy." He turned the other way to mimic a birdshow host, "Why do you say that, Risa?" He turned back to imitate Risa, "Because Olive the parts weren't there, hee, hee, hee!"

"C'mon, Caspar, that's not funny, huh, huh, huh."

"Well, you aren't the only one with jokes, Risa." Caspar made a funny face and changed his voice, leaning to one side, "So, Risa, we all heard you scream like a little girl that night. Was it really so bad, or do you just like screaming?" He turned to the other side to mimic Risa, "It was really gross, Mr. Macaw. Like when someone hits a dead bird with a lawnmower—ooo, ooo, ooo! Sorry, Mr. Macaw!" Caspar continued as the bird-show host, "I guess that might make me scream like a little girl, too, Risa. I'm not sure."

"Har, hardy, har. You can laugh and make jokes all you like, tee, hee, hee," Risa hung his shaking head and began to shuffle away. "It was awful and I don't ever want to see any-thing like it again—bird shows or no bird shows."

Hope's compassionate gaze followed him a moment before she also turned toward home. "Maybe none of us will have to see anything like that again."

XXVII

SOME animals listened to the bird shows religiously. Some only listened to hear the weather guess. Others only listened when there was new, exciting information. These latter animals had long since stopped listening after Risa's discovery of the slain animal, but that was about to change.

"So, based on that weather guess, we'd better stay close to those caves, pad those beds and nests, and fluff out those feathers. Thank you, Phil. And now—"

"Just a minute, Tina, I understand we have some late-breaking information. Sam, are you there? Can you hear me Sam?"

"Yes I can, Bill," came the answer from a stork standing across the sidewalk from the bird show. "Bill, Tina, I am saddened to report that there has been another violent attack here in the Animal Zoo. All we know at this time is that a terrible fight occurred today between a public safety officer and a young animal, and both are currently in the infirmary as a result. The authorities have not released anything further at this time."

Before long, the animals who listened to the bird shows constantly had spread the news to those who listened infrequently. The number of animals watching the shows swelled again. Although neither of the fight participants was in any condition to speak out, there were a number of witnesses who had seen the conflagration.

"Now, ma'am, you say you were present as this tragic event unfolded?"

"That's right; I was standing right over there picking lice out of Marie's hair when I says, 'Marie, lookit there! That mountain line jus' jumped that li'l rhino mindin' his own bid'ness,' an she says to me, 'Lawdy!'"

"Did you see what transpired, ma'am?"

"Yes I did, Alex. This young ruffian rhino—looked like a clan member to me—well he was over there by that, over kinda there, and he was acting very suspicious-like. And all of us are scared after what happened last week, what's a lady to do what with all these scofflaws? So, we called over to this nice public safety officer—a mountain lion, he was—and as soon as he approached the miscreant, that terrible thing attacked him! You can't even treat them like respectable animals. They're terrible, Alex!"

Each time a new bit of information emerged, it ignited a succession of flurries of excitement around the bird shows.

"... We have just learned, Terry, that the young rhino was, in fact, a clan member ..."

"... an unnamed source in the infirmary has confirmed that the officer has older injuries that could have been obtained in the recent tragedy ..."

"... public safety records indicate that the officer in this altercation has been sanctioned by the leaders for aggressive behavior in the past ..."

"... representatives of one of the clans—speaking under conditions of anonymity—have admitted that the injured rhino has previously demonstrated problems with authority figures ..."

The excitement and differences of opinion were not limited to the bird shows. In every corner of the zoo, animals debated whether officers abused their authority, whether clans had become too violent to tolerate, and whether some animals were wrongly being treated differently than others. Risa was just relieved that he was being left alone since the bird shows had something else to focus on.

BOOK FIVE

GORDO

XXVIII

OLD Slylock loved the teaching opportunities that big events in the zoo presented. He had been teaching the history of the Animal Zoo, and now he had the chance to discuss the establishment of the magistrates.

"Can anyone tell me what the magistrates do? Yes, Riki?"

The mongoose fidgeted while answering, "They decide arguments between animals about stuff."

"Yes, Riki, that's one thing they do. Can anyone tell me another? Yes, Babe?"

A young water buffalo with a smoky blue coat answered while his lengthy tongue probed one of his cavernous, drippy nostrils. "They also decide if someone did something wrong."

"That's absolutely right, Babe. And we should have a great example of the magistrates deciding if someone did something wrong very shortly. Has anyone seen the bird shows? Does anyone know what I'm talking about?" Slylock's beady eyes surveyed the class. "Yes, Faith?"

"Do you mean the mountain lion and the rhino that fought?"

"That's right, Faith. Very likely, both will face the magistrate, who will determine if one of them did something wrong. Now," he swished his tail hypnotically, "since we've been talking about the wonderful changes the animals who moved here from the Old Country made, can anyone tell me how it will be better for these two here, versus how they would have fared there?"

Slylock happily surmised that none of his pupils had any opinion he would have to overcome. Instead, they all awaited his superior knowledge. His pacing exuded confidence, and his swishy tail became as convincing as ever. "Back in the Old Country, the rhino might have been found to be wrong and even punished, primarily because he was not a lion! Can you imagine?"

Gasps of astonishment pervaded the class, which was markedly devoid of great cats.

"And the public safety officer," continued Slylock, "would have been found innocent of wrongdoing, simply because he was a lion!"

"No!"

"That's awful!"

"It is awful. So when the patriarchs founded the Animal Zoological Gardens of Eden, they wanted to prevent that kind of unfairness from happening here. That is why they wrote two of our most important rules in the Animal Zoo Charter. The first, that magistrates are selected by the leaders. That way they shouldn't be swayed to make unfair decisions in order to please the animals voting in the selections. The other very important rule is that all animals must be treated equally by the magistrates. It doesn't matter if they are lions, or rhinos, or mongooses, or water buffalos, or whomever: the magistrates must treat all animals equally. Doesn't that all make you glad you live in the Animal Zoo rather than the Old Country?"

The little animals who heard him to the end agreed unanimously, but a handful failed to hear him quite to the end. They had doubts. Behind furrowed brows they tried to decide if a real difference existed between the Old Country and the Animal Zoo in this area. They wondered if leaders choosing magistrates in the zoo would necessarily result in fairer outcomes than leaders choosing magistrates in the Old Country. These few decided to watch and see.

XXIX

THE chief magistrate in the Animal Zoo was Gordo, a phenomenally obese orangutan who was more at home in leonine social circles than in primate. He wore old wire-frame glasses perched on his ample nose to lend him a distinguished air. Somewhere behind these glasses he presumably had eyes, but they were so deeply embedded in rolls of fat that they could not be seen.

Gordo's assistant was a ferret named Snivel. He had told the birds that his magisterial eminence, Gordo, would announce a key development at noon. Experience had taught the birds that the chief magistrate would be fashionably late; however, they were loathe to miss anything important, so they gathered en masse at the appointed time.

At about half past noon, basking in self-important glory, Gordo appeared behind his assistant. Snivel pompously announced in redundancy that his eminence was present to make a statement.

Eager to give the appearance of having other important matters to attend to, Gordo did not beat around the bush. "I have been in conference with Diablo, the Animal Zoo Accuser. He intends to bring both participants in the recent fight to me for a determination of wrongdoing. Witnesses should expect to be interviewed by Diablo. Other than that, keep quiet. I don't want anyone's memory being influenced by loose talk. Understood? Good!"

Then Gordo turned his impressive bulk and waddled laboriously back indoors, leaving Snivel to deal with the birds and their questions. The birds fired questions at Snivel like a machine gun:

"Will both participants have their determinations at the same time?"

"Are there advocates on the case yet?"

"When will the determinations be held?"

"Will the two be held until determination, or allowed out?"

"Have they recovered enough to make statements?"

Although the onslaught was intense, Snivel deftly dodged all the questions with either, "You heard His Eminence," or "That has not been decided at this time." When one of these responses didn't seem to fit the question, Snivel made it seem that his response was meant for a different bird's question.

After a few minutes, he dismissed the crowds, assuring them that he would let them know whenever he had new information.

N EW information did surface, and when it did, it involved the advocates. Johnny Claw, the public safety officer, had used his resources and connections to engage the services of Stinkmeyer, Funk, and Spray, the most prominent, prestigious advocates in the Gardens.

Stinkmeyer, Funk, and Spray individually were skunks, and among the most well-fed inhabitants of the Animal Zoo. Their coats were among the sleekest, their eyes among the sharpest, their nails among the best kempt. These three employed a myriad of skunks, weasels, and minks as assistants and information gatherers. These employees almost always found whatever evidence or witnesses their client needed, simply due to the large amount of resources at their disposal. Stinkmeyer, Funk, and Spray never lost.

At the same time, Forty, the black rhino, having neither the resources nor the connections that the lion did, was forced to utilize Toupée, the volunteer advocate. Toupée was an almost entirely stationary tree sloth, who picked up his name as a baby when he was once mistaken for an entirely stationary lost hair piece lying on the ground. Since that occasion, he had changed somewhat. Now he would never be mistaken for a lost hair piece on the ground, but he might be mistaken for an overgrown and horribly soiled hair piece lost up in a tree.

Toupée had one assistant, Lichen, an opossum who was only nominally more active than himself. Lichen would never be counted on to pursue a client's interests quite as diligently as he pursued midnight scraps from the garbage heap. The volunteer advocate and his assistant rarely won anything.

The bird shows were abuzz with the news. "This is an interesting development, Stan."

"Yes it is, Vicki. I'm sure we all remember the past successes Stinkmeyer, Funk, and Spray have enjoyed. In particular, many of you will recall when they represented Tang —"

"Wasn't that the tiger suspected of the gruesome killing of a giraffe in McArthur Park a while back, Stan?"

"That's right, Vicki. Remember the giraffe's neck was nearly bitten in two in multiple places, and Stinkmeyer maneuvered Diablo the accuser into asking Tang to demonstrate biting a mock-up of a giraffe neck—"

"Oh, yes! I remember! Tang pretended he couldn't even get his mouth around the fake giraffe neck! 'If the neck ain't bit, you must aquit,' Stinkmeyer said."

"Well, Vicki, no one really knows if he was pretending, but I wonder if we can hope for something as brilliant from Stinkmeyer, Funk, and Spray in this case!"

"Only time will tell, Stan. And what can we expect to see out of Toupée and Lichen—"

"Or will we see anything at all, Vicki? So many of their clients simply claim responsibility, you have to wonder if that's what Forty is planning."

"I guess if you expect to be found responsible regardless, Stan, why go to such great expense with advocates like Stinkmeyer?"

"That makes sense, Vicki. I can't wait to see this play out. Next, we'll be going over to Wanda for her weather guess. What have you got for us, Wanda?"

"ALRIGHT, class, one final topic for today. Do you remember our discussion about magistrates, and how they are required to treat all animals equally? And that," Slylock continued, pacing confidently, "is why both Forty the rhino and Johnny Claw the mountain lion will be examined for responsibility.

"Have you seen the bird shows? Both Forty and Johnny Claw will have advocates to assist them during the determination. Of course, I don't think it would, but if something like this happened and some of you were involved, wouldn't this fairness and equality make you glad you live here in the Animal Zoo instead of in the Old Country?"

The students readily agreed that fairness with the magistrates and the assistance of advocates were infinitely better than facing caprice and favoritism all alone. They swelled with pride at the superiority of their zoological gardens.

Slylock sensed the increase in their boisterousness due to having sat through long and tedious studies, so he decided it was a perfect time for their daily recitation of the Animal Zoo creed. As usual, they turned the recitation into an unspoken contest of who could express animalism the loudest and most fervently. Slylock beamed with pride himself as his students recited:

"We owe our allegiance, And our lives,
To the Animal Zoological Gardens of Eden
And to the ideals,
For which it stands,
Equality, opportunity, truth, and fairness,
For every animal, type, and species."

XXXII

DURING the ensuing days, nothing in the gardens could overcome the excitement of the determination. Gordo made public appearances wherein he waddled impressively and shifted his bulk gloriously. His disproportionately long orangutan arms went from rest, to snaking away from him at either side, to flying about, gesticulating animatedly and pointing furiously. His sycophantic toady, Snivel, seemed to be two separate creatures, the fore and aft ends of the lengthy ferret independently running here and there from the accuser to the advocates and back to the magistrate.

Forty the rhino and Johnny Claw the mountain lion made their first public appearance since the fight, causing a great stir. Both were still heavily bandaged in a number of places, both walked closely with their advocates, and both maintained silence when the birds began their ceaseless onslaught of questions.

All three of the famous skunks advocating for Johnny Claw sat with him at a table, which seemed lost under a mountain of important-looking papers and folders. Just behind them, in the general seating area, a half-dozen assistants scribbled frantically, or leaned forward to whisper to one of the prestigious polecats. Johnny Claw himself sat motionless, giving every impression of respectability and forbearance, the very impression that his advocates had painstakingly coached him to give.

At a second table, Toupée gave every impression of having fallen irretrievably into an eternal coma. His assistant, Lichen, gave such a believable impression of being dead that fat bottle flies even landed on him, deceived into believing him to be deceased, and to have been deceased long enough to provide a prime location to harbor their precious little maggots. Forty, looking big, dark, and belligerent, occupied a seat beside his advocates.

At a third table sat Diablo, the accuser. Diablo was a howler monkey. All his assistant accusers were howler monkeys. Their booming accusatory cries could be heard reverberating all over the zoo at any given moment of any given day, regardless whether there was a determination in progress or not:

"YOOO-OOO! YOOO-OOO! YOOO-OOO!"

"YOOO-OOO! YOOO!"

"YOOO-OOO! YOOO-OOO! YOOO!"

The accusers had long, thin, hairy arms shooting out at odd angles from their squat, hairy bodies. Their surrealistically spindly arms were tipped with equally surrealistically spider-like fingers, which the accusers would point at anyone and everyone while whooping their echoing accusations.

Once the determinations started, some witnesses to the confrontation told what they remembered seeing. Other witnesses telling what they remembered, shared the exact opposite views. Meanwhile, Diablo and his assistants swung around the entire determination area indiscriminately whooping at everyone assembled:

"YOOO-OOO! YOOO!"

"YOOO-OOO! YOOO-OOO! YOOO!"

"YOOO-OOO! YOOO-OOO! YOOO-OOO!"

"YOOO-OOO! YOOO!"

"YOOO-OOO! YOOO-OOO! YOOO!"

They whooped, jabbing bony fingers at witnesses, Gordo, Forty, Johnny Claw, the birds, in short, everyone. They swung over so much of the area, and swooped so fluidly and continually that the determination had the appearance of a grandfather clock shop with all the pendulums in syncopated motion simultaneously.

The antics of the accuser and his assistants were so powerful and disconcerting that everyone present felt somewhat guilty of something, just on general principle.

With each witness, eventually Diablo's swinging, finger-pointing, and accusatorial YOOO-whooping wound down, as he and his assistants returned to their places. Then, either Stinkmeyer, Funk, or Spray would rise in solemn dignity, select an important-looking paper or two from the table, and then glide elegantly over to question the animal. Each would stop to scratch his head or stroke his chin while appearing to study something unseen on the paper. With a squinting eye and tilted head, he would ask the witness, "Are you quite sure?" He would then confer with the other advocates or assistants, repeating these actions until most witnesses were no longer sure of what they'd seen, or even what they'd just said that they'd seen.

After Johnny Claw's advocates were finished questioning each witness, Gordo gave Toupée the same opportunity. Each time, an almost imperceptible movement, detectable only by the magistrate's trained eye, signified that the public advocate had no additional inquiries.

Each day—even each break in the proceedings in a given day—found the bird shows tittering endlessly about what had transpired and what the developments meant for Forty and Johnny Claw. The birds explained the proceedings, they evaluated the magistrate, and they critiqued the advocates. They brought out experts to hash and rehash everything the birds had just pre-hashed, and to make predictions about the eventual outcome.

Most of the experts made comments and forecasts based

on their personal opinions about justice rather than the way the evidence and testimony indicated. Former advocates were convinced, for example, that neither had done wrong. Former accusers were certain that they had both done wrong, and went on to accuse the birds and all the audience members as well.

Finally, the birds interviewed dozens of ordinary animals to get their opinions. The birds asked them what had occurred that fateful night, regardless whether they had been present. And they asked them what a fair result of the determination would be, regardless whether they had been present to see or hear any of the evidence or testimony.

XXXIII

THE determination having been made, the bird shows ushered in the aftermath. A spectacularly colored peacock flashed his entire plumage to its maximum brilliance as he shrieked a controversial question over the squawking of the other birds:

"Was your decision influenced by the fact that Forty is a dark-colored animal, whereas Johnny Claw is a light-colored animal?"

His Eminence, Chief Magistrate Gordo, appeared to swell to the point just before the point of physically exploding as he roared, "OF COURSE NOT! My determination of responsibility follows the evidence and eyewitness testimony! Not to mention that your colorist suggestion ignores the fact that Johnny Claw's advocates were dark-colored! Don't be ridiculous!"

But no matter how Gordo shouted, or jiggled his jowls, or wildly flailed his absurdly long arms, most of the bird shows focused on the fact that he found the light-colored animal not responsible of wrong doing, while he found the dark-colored animal responsible.

Toupée and Lichen were unable to be roused for a comment. Stinkmeyer, Funk, and Spray presented a very articulate, prepared statement commending Gordo for the fairness of his determination. They praised him for—in their words—"following the evidence and witness testimony to arrive at the only possible just result."

Many animals protested the decision. They appeared on bird shows brutally condemning the magistrate, the system, and all light-colored animals, whether they were involved in any way or not.

Mahomet, a dark-colored camel spider, used this opportunity to call for an all-out war, attempting to goad members of his clan to act toward that end. Jesse, a bug-eyed chameleon that could be any color convenient to him at the moment, chose dark for this occasion and harped about the oppression he and "his fellow dark-colored animals" had endured. He lambasted the practice of animals having to work for other animals, though that practice had been abolished from the zoo generations before he had hatched. Conya, a black bear that entertained other animals by juggling or dancing on a ball, complained of discrimination, saying that all the public safety officers, magistrates, and leaders were light-colored, whereas all the victims of their abuses were dark-colored. This belied the clear fact that a great percentage of the officers, magistrates, and leaders were dark-colored. He ignored jaguars, wolverines, alligators, carnivorous apes, and even bears like himself.

Since the bird shows gave more credence to ideology and opinion than actual facts, the hosts commiserated, shaking their heads and making sad eyes during these comments. If any animal tried to introduce facts contrary to the opinions being voiced, the hosts shrieked and squawked them to silence while berating them for insensitivity and hate. No animal—they stated—should have his or her opinions subjected to such harsh, unsympathetic, and obviously colorist criticism. They failed to recognize their inconsistency in this.

XXXIV

SLYLOCK saw the raised hand on her stubby arm and called on Charity.

"I'm still having a little trouble seeing how that was equal treatment," she cooed through a scrunched up koala face. "I talked to my parents, and I saw some of the bird shows about the determination. It just doesn't seem equal when Officer Johnny Claw's advocates were so good, so smart, so clever, and so professional. But poor Forty! His advocates kept falling asleep, and they didn't do anything to help him. Not anything at all! That's not fair or equal!"

Old Slylock was stalling for time throughout Charity's question, which was the reason he even let her speak at such length to begin with. He paced slowly, swishing his tail hypnotically to divert attention from the frantic darting of his beady little eyes.

"Yes, well, I imagine, young Charity," he drawled, "that since you are one of my brightest pupils—although all of you are bright and hard-working, aren't you?" His mouth spewed this stream of dribble automatically while he racked his brain for an answer. "Since you are one of my brightest pupils, as I was saying, had you only thought about it a little harder, or perhaps a little longer, you may have found the very answer you're looking for. That is why, my precious students, I always encourage you to think things through for yourselves. You may not have me around forever, after all, but I still want you to think properly as I have taught you, and to come to the right conclusions I have given to you."

Slylock's pacing left him mostly facing toward either side of the students rather than at them, so they noticed no change in his demeanor; but there was one nonetheless. A visible wave of relief passed momentarily over his spastic eyes as the solution came to him.

"Of course, the determination was fair. It could not have been any other way. Fairness is what makes the Animal Zoological Gardens of Eden so much better than anywhere else in the world where you could live. If we didn't have such fairness, we wouldn't be as great as I keep explaining to you we are.

"Consider this: Officer Johnny Claw was able to engage the advocates Stinkmeyer, Funk, and Spray because of his resources and his connections, something Forty didn't have, right? Now, if somehow they had both been given the same advocate—either Stinkmeyer or Toupée, for example—then there would be no recognition or benefit for Officer Claw's greater resources and connections, things he must have worked very hard for, correct?

"And then, carrying this idea to its logical end," Slylock's pacing and tail swishing were now accompanied with confident, dancing eyes, "someone in a system like that could be poor and lazy and offensive and unfriendly, yet still receive the same quality of advocacy. That would not be fair or equal, Charity, to take away the benefit Officer Claw has earned by working for greater resources and connections. In fact, to give him the same level of advocacy as Forty—who had done nothing we know of to earn it—would be like stealing something from him! Would any of you think it was fair or equal if Officer Claw had something stolen from him, and Forty the rhino did not?"

While the students generally roared their disapproval of such hypothetical injustice, Charity furrowed her brow, trying to figure out why something in Slylock's explanation still seemed wrong to her.

BOOK SIX
CASPAR

XXXV

THE area was curiously vacant around Caspar and his family as they strolled. It didn't matter where they went or why, the buffer zone between them and other animals was substantial. Sometimes even greater, depending on the direction of the wind.

"Pops, wouldn't it be cool to be king?" Caspar's gaze joined his father's upturned face, towards the clouds.

"King?" his father grunted.

"Yeah, you could always do whatever you wanted, eat whatever you wanted, go wherever you wanted. You could fart and nobody would say anything about it. In fact, they'd all probably crawl all over each other trying to out-compliment one another, telling you how great you smell. All that just to get on your good side! They'd all be afraid to laugh at you or make fun of you.

"Even waddling would become popular, instead of something everyone made fun of. Short tails sticking up would be 'in' while long, hangy, floppy ones would be 'out'. Crazy tusky teeth would be a sign of nobility. Crazier the better! Everyone would respect a good sense of smell more than height, trunks, or claws—"

"Son, I don't know why you're worried about all that," his mother said. "You don't have to be a king to be happy with who you are."

"And it isn't like you can change things, boy," his father added. "Lions are kings. We're just warthogs. We like mud and stinky food. Take us as we are or leave us, I always say. We're fun and fun-loving. Most of those other animals are too stuffy for me, I always say." He accented his own lack of stuffiness with a long-winded belch, beaming tuskily from ear to ear. "Where did you come up with the idea of being king anyway? Have those other kids been picking on you or something?"

"No, Pops, nothing like that. We just learned in school that a handful of farms in the world are ruled by pigs. That got me thinking how cool it would be to live someplace like that, to be like a king. Don't you think that would be cool?"

"I dunno, son. I hadn't really thought about it. But I'm sure there's good and bad in it, as I always say."

"Good and bad in it? I don't get what that even means."

"Maybe it would help if I told you a story to show you what I mean ... "

XXXVI

"SON," Caspar's father began, his throaty voice emerging from the motley collection of misshapen tusks lining his unsightly snout, "sometimes things aren't as good or bad as they seem at first, I always say. This story will show you what I mean.

"A long time ago, way off in Africa, there lived a fat, tusky little warthog—the pride of his sow and boar. A stinkier little pig no one ever saw. One day, he came upon a huge beehive brimming with the sweetest honey imaginable. He ate his fill, and then ate some more for good measure. What would you say about that?"

"That's great!" Caspar drooled, licking his lips wistfully.

"Well, maybe it was and maybe it wasn't. You see, he ate so quickly that he paid no attention to whether all the honey he ate was green or cured, and he ate so much of it that it made him very sick to his stomach. He was so sick that he threw up until his stomach and sides were terribly sore, and he'd made an awful mess everywhere. His boar frowned and his sow told him to clean up the mess. What would you say about that?"

"That's awful!" Caspar said, holding his pot belly sympathetically.

"Well, maybe it was and maybe it wasn't. As it turned out, the bees had built their hive around a golden necklace that someone had lost. In his hurry to eat the honey, the little pig had not seen it and had eaten it. It came up when he got sick, and he found it while cleaning up the mess. What would you say about that?"

"That's good!" the wide-eyed Caspar exclaimed.

"Well, maybe it was and maybe it wasn't. The little warthog cleaned the necklace until it shined like new. He began wearing it everywhere. It was so bright and shiny that it attracted a lot of attention. One day a cheetah saw the glinting gold and chased the pig, who ran as fast as his feet would carry him. In fact, he ran so quickly he couldn't stop, and both he and the cheetah fell over a ledge overhanging a tumultuous river. What would you say about that?"

"That's horrible!" shrieked Caspar, skipping in a circle as if he was the one being chased by a cheetah.

"Maybe it was and maybe it wasn't. Though the necklace attracted the cheetah, it caught on a branch as the warthog fell toward the raging river. He hung there as the cheetah fell helplessly into the river, and he was just able to climb back onto the top of the ledge safely. What do you think of that?"

"Whew! That's great!" Caspar blew out in relief. "What happened after THAT?"

"After that? I don't really remember. The point is, things aren't always as they seem. Don't jump to conclusions about whether something is good or bad, as I always say. It might be a mixture of both, or even the opposite of what it seems at first."

XXXVII

SEVERAL exhausted little animals lay under the spreading branches in the shade of a large oak tree. While their bodies rested from playing tag and capture the flag, their minds wandered.

"What do you think it would be like to have pigs as kings?" Caspar mused.

"Stinky."

"Smelly."

"Sweaty, too." His friends answered.

"C'mon, guys, seriously!"

"Alright, Caspar," began Hope. "You heard Ol' Sly in class. In the Animal Farm they had pig leaders who were like kings, and it was all bad. They had wanted something better, so they started off like our Animal Zoo—"

"Yeah, hee, hee, hee," Risa butted in, "lots of talk about equality and truth and justice and all-for-one and one-for-all. But then it changed for them didn't it? Eventually it was just like under the lion kings, equality for some, justice for some, a few taking everything for themselves and leaving scraps and leftovers for all the other animals."

Slylock would have been proud of how thoroughly his students had absorbed what he had taught.

"It seems like to me it would probably suck just as bad in the Animal Farm as in the Old Country under lion kings," Faith put in.

"Boy, are we ever lucky!"

"I'll say!" chimed in the others.

"What I don't get is how those animals could be so stupid. I mean, couldn't they see what was happening? I'd expect the sheep to just hopelessly give up and take whatever the pigs dished out—"

"And maybe the lemmings, if they had any, heh, he, he, I'd expect them to go along with the crowd, hah, ha, ha!"

"Right, Risa, but what about all the others?" Hope asked. "Why let themselves be treated that way?"

"Maybe it changed so slowly that they didn't even notice how bad it had gotten," hummed Charity. "Kind of like how we don't notice getting hot and tired until it really hits us."

"Maybe so."

Finally, refreshed sufficiently, the little animals were happy to drop their mental exercise and return to play. Soon they were running and shrieking happily around the grassy area again, little caring whether lion kings or pigs or leaders ruled.

XXXVIII

SINCE the grassy area where the little animals were playing was located across the zoo from where they lived, they had to cross other areas to reach their homes. They became very quiet while passing another clearing. This clearing was encircled by lush flowers, and it had a beautiful white gazebo. A number of small animals were playing in this clearing as well.

"Look at that ball," Caspar sighed.

"Way nicer than anything we ever get," Hope whispered.

Various little animals murmured their agreement, but then all were astonished when an angry young lioness ripped through the ball with her claws. She emphasized whatever point she was arguing by violently slinging the torn ball into the woods beyond the flower beds.

While some of her peers continued to argue with her, others turned back to their game. One pulled an identical new ball from the bushes around the gazebo where Caspar and his friends hadn't seen it previously.

"Did you see that?" he hissed. "They don't just have one ball nicer than anything we have, they've got more!"

"And they can afford to destroy them over a silly argument, and just play with another one!" Hope added.

"If I ever had anything that nice you could bet I'd take better care of it than that!" moaned Caspar.

"Hoo, ho, ho, I'd be happy with the torn-up one that they threw into the woods," said Risa. "I bet we could patch it up or—"

"Say, do you think we could get it? Do you think they'd care?" Faith said, craning her neck trying to see the damaged ball.

Caspar and his friends had gotten so excited over the fine toys the lion cubs had that they had stopped walking altogether. They stood in a clump, talking in hushed tones. They were so engrossed in their discussion and so focused on the possibility of getting the damaged ball that none of them even noticed when the new ball the other animals were playing with rolled over near them. Nor did they notice when one of the other animals came skipping over to get it.

"U M ... what're you guys doing?" asked the young lion. Though he had been running and playing, his rugged good looks and charm were in no way affected.

Caspar, Faith, and the others muttered and shuffled their feet. They looked down. They scratched themselves. The lion cub kicked the ball into the air to himself a couple of times, then he effortlessly flung it far back into the clearing where his companions were waiting.

"Whoa! What's that awful smell? Somebody step in something, or did one of you do that?" The lion still grinned winningly through the mild rebuke.

More muttering and shuffling accompanied nods and other non-verbal indications toward Caspar, who blushed as deeply as possible for a warthog. He had never felt so embarrassed.

"Where do you guys come from? I've never seen you at school or anything," the cub asked.

Faith hunched down so much she blended in with her shorter friends as she answered, "we go to school over by where we live ... across the mini-train tracks from here."

The other animals with her fed off her relative confidence enough to emerge slightly, gesturing to indicate the general direction of their homes and school.

"Mr. Slylock is our teacher—"

"We call him Ol' Sly—"

"He's a fox—"

"He must be about a hundred years old—"

"Wait, wait," cut in the young lion. "You guys all have the same teacher? But there's so many of you!"

A puzzled Caspar responded, "All of us? He's the teacher for our whole school. There's even more in his class than this!"

"What? Our school has lots of teachers! How can all of you have just one teacher?"

By now, their fears abated by familiarity without adverse effect, all the little animals from across the tracks became experts.

"We all sit around together in one class—"

"Actually, there's a lot more of us than this—"

"Most of us aren't even here—"

"And your teacher tries to teach all of you?" asked the cub. "How do any of you get enough time with him to learn anything?"

"We all just sit there and learn together—"

"We're all there—"

"Yup, that's right, we're all there—"

"And he just talks to us about stuff—"

"But wait a minute," the good-natured cub shook his head. "Everyone's different, so you can't learn exactly the same way can you? You eat different foods, walk differently, and make different sounds. Why would you expect to learn the same way?" The young lion's logical comparisons and reasoning easily won the other animals' agreement. They voiced their concurrence and nodded as he continued, "In our school, we have several teachers. Each one teaches two or three of us who learn in a similar way. That way we're able to get more benefit when we ask questions or go special places or do special things, or when we try things for ourselves, like experiments."

"Go places?—"

"See things?—"

"Experi-what?—"

"We don't do any of that at our school!"

As dusk approached, the animals from the other side of the mini-train tracks had to begin heading home. Caspar turned the conversation to what many of his friends were thinking, "Say, what's going to happen to that ball in the woods?"

"What do you mean?" the cub replied. "The old torn-up one that Nala clawed and threw there? I don't know. I guess nothing. Why?"

The other animals, anticipating success, brightened, "Can we have it?"

"I guess so. I don't know why you'd want it, though. She tore it."

Caspar and his friends didn't hear anything after, 'I guess so.' They were already racing off to find the torn ball as fast as their various little legs would carry them.

The little lion shook his head, turning back toward where his peers were playing. "I wonder what that was all about. I wonder why they don't just get a new ball like we did. Strange."

XL

CASPAR'S mother noticed something was amiss when she saw him chew his food distractedly, rather than pigging it down noisily. Normally, he inhaled his food unchewed, eyeballed his siblings' portions hungrily, and occasionally snuck some from them. She couldn't imagine what would cause him enough anxiety to put him off his dinner.

"Hey, Mom?"

"Yes, Caspar?"

"Are there a bunch of different schools in the zoo?"

Even though she hadn't known what was bothering him, this question still came as a surprise to her. "Why do you ask that, dear?"

"Well, we met this lion cub as we were walking home today. He was telling us all about his school. I just wondered if the zoo had more schools I didn't know about."

"Oh, I'm sure there are a few. What makes you so interested in the other schools?"

"Well see, this lion cub, he was telling us about his school." Caspar's younger siblings took advantage of him being distracted and finished off his dinner for a change while he continued, "They have lots of teachers, and they get to go on learning trips. They even get to do experiments and everything. It just sounded so interesting and fun compared with Ol' Sly."

His mother tried to mask the sadness in her voice, "Caspar, that might be one way to learn, but you can always learn by trying hard and applying yourself at your school, too."

"But why can't my school be more like his? We're all in the same zoo, why can't our schools be the same? Aren't all animals supposed to be equal and everything?"

"A lot about a school has to do with where you live, Caspar. We just have to learn to do the best we can with what we have."

"If we had pigs for kings, I'd try to be king, and I'd make sure we had as good a school as any other animal!"

"I'm sure you'd make a fine king, or leader for that matter. Now go play!"

She tousled his head with a quick maternal noogie as he sprang off to join his giggly, full siblings.

BOOK SEVEN
PRINCE

XLI

FOLLOWING his encounter with the young animals from the other side of the mini-train tracks, the lion cub had a few questions for his father, Rey, the reigning Lord-mayor of the zoo.

"Dad?"

"Yes, Prince?"

"I met some animals from the other side of the zoo today—"

"Did you?"

"Yes, and they were telling me about their school. Are all the other schools in the gardens as different from mine as that?"

"I don't know what they told you, son, but schools can be a bit different, I suppose. Some of the differences are due to where the school is. If a school is in a better area, it must become a better school. The tree growing in better dirt and in a sunnier spot will grow greener, taller, and stronger, will it not?"

"I guess so, Dad."

"Additionally, a school can only move at the pace of its students. You attend a school with the best and brightest animals in the zoological gardens, animals all destined for greatness, leaders in the making. Of course, your school will have an atmosphere more attuned to learning and excelling. What do you think is going on at those other schools?"

"I don't know—"

"I'd imagine they spend class time primarily digging in their noses and sniffing each others' rear ends! I'm sure their teachers—"

"Teacher—"

"I'm sure their teacher could give them the educational equivalent of your school if he or she didn't have to spend all day wiping snotty noses, correcting bad hygiene, and refocusing students obsessed with scratching themselves!"

"Maybe so, Dad. They didn't seem so bad, but maybe I just don't know as much about it as you. They certainly were quick to go dig up a stinking busted old ball out of the woods instead of just getting a new one."

"You see what I mean, son? They just aren't ready for the same level of education. They aren't ready to be leaders, to run things the way animals like us do."

"But can't any animal—even one of those from other areas of the zoo—become a leader by being selected, just like you were?"

"Technically, that's correct, son. Thank goodness there's a little more to it than that: I can't imagine what would happen if one of them ever was selected!"

XLII

"DAD, what do you mean when you say, 'There's more to it than that'? I thought the Animal Zoo was built on equality for all animals. And that equality is guaranteed in part by letting all animals select the leaders, and in part by permitting all animals to try for selection, right?"

"Ho, ho, ho!" Prince's father's laugh was warm, deep, and genuine. Prince's charm and natural good looks undoubtedly came from his father: every animal's animal.

"Prince, you're learning well, but again, there is more to it than that. Remember what we were saying about the animals on the other side of the mini-train tracks? Droolers, no wait, it was nose-pickers and butt-sniffers, right? Ho, ho, ho! No matter, tongue-draggers, mouth-breathers, slobber-jaws, they're all the same.

"You see, son, many animals just aren't cut out to be leaders. They wouldn't do what was best for the whole zoo—not that they wouldn't mean well. But how could they do what's best, really? They come from schools that didn't prepare them. They come from families that only care about their next meal or having babies—"

"But, dad, even if they are all those things you say, they can still try to be selected, right?"

"Oh, sure, they can try, Prince. But without the resources to win support, without the education necessary to speak competently, without a leader's appearance, and without the support of other leaders, no one would select them!"

"But then there isn't equality! It's the same as the Old Country where then animals had no say."

"Whoa! Whoa! Ho, ho, ho! Not so fast, son. Those are strong accusations!" Rey mock-frowned, then smiled. "There is still equality for all animals. Every animal gets roughly what he or she deserves. Some of us are born and bred for greatness. We have resources, connections, and education. It would be completely unfair and unequal to throw all that away and have us take our marching orders from butt-sniffers, droolers, and mouth-breathers who can't think beyond their next meal. We're all moving forward equally—from where we start. We don't start off equal in the world, and it would be unfair and unequal if those starting at the bottom—pardon the pun! Ho, ho!—advanced farther or faster than those above them. Does that make sense to you?"

"I guess so. When you say it like that."

"It should make sense: it works. Did you know that because of the huge successes of our own Animal Zoo, similar animal zoological gardens have been established all over the world? They've almost completely replaced the inferior system from the Old Country."

"But what about the Animal Farms? Other kinds of animals lead them, right?"

"Horrible! In every case the lesser animals murdered or exiled their leaders. But it became clear over the years how incapable the lesser animals were at leading—filthy swine! What a joke! The animals on those farms go hungry while the pigs steal them blind. They started with talk of fairness and equality, but they didn't finish it with action! Here in the Animal Zoological Gardens of Eden, we did!"

XLIII

PRINCE'S curiosity was still piqued by the things his father had said, so he discussed them with the other two students in his personalized study team. They all agreed to share their newly aroused interest with some of their teachers.

Their leadership teacher was an old, grey lion, who still retained a dignified air despite having the happy eyes, warm smile, and ready laugh of a grandfather. He had served the zoo in a number of leadership positions, and had then retired to teach a new generation of leaders. He took Prince and his fellow pupils to meet an actual great-granddaughter of Snowball, one of the original revolutionary leaders of the Animal Farm. She was a fat, old sow, nearly blind, living in a rarely visited corner of the zoo. Despite her humble appearance and modest dwelling, she was a phenomenal storyteller who wove a moral into every tale.

"Yes, children," she seemed to wink at them, though one could never be sure if her eyes were actually more open or less open due to the fat rolls in which they were sunk, "I still remember my great-grandfather fretting: 'Kasha,' he called me porridge, you see, 'Kasha, after zhat brute chase me from zee farm, why don't others send for me? I know zhose thugs have make life terrible for all zee animals—why they not call me back?' But zhat is zee way of zee power, children: no one readily give up zee power. And anozher zhing you beware yourself: someone who seek to obtain zee power wizh you, will eventually seek to take zee power from you ... mmm, indeed."

The young animals left the interview knowing more about the original Animal Farm and the farm way of life than most animals living in one. They decided to ask their history teacher if she had any ideas about how to learn more about the Old Country lion kings.

The history teacher for Prince and his peers was a tigress not many years older than themselves. Her exotic coat was one of the most beautiful in the whole zoo, and she seemed to purr almost every word. Naturally, all the male students maintained a perpetual crush on her. She pretended to be oblivious to this fact, but she rarely lost an opportunity to enflame them further with just the right tilt of her head, or the slowest blink of her deep, orange and black eyes, or the most alluring flick of her luxurious tail. On this occasion, she assured Prince and the others that she knew just the person to help find the answers they were looking for, and she sent their pulses racing with a winning smile.

Not long afterward she sashayed into the world of primates with her pupils in rapt attention behind her to find the individual she was certain could tell them about the lion kings better than any other.

"So, you've actually SEEN a lion king?" Prince's eyes widened as he leaned forward expectantly.

"Hoo-yah bah-yah, lotsa times-yah," answered the ancient, grey-haired baboon rhythmically. His rheumy eyes never left his odd collection of tiny trinkets and bones as he cast them on the ground, studied them, or scooped them up for another throw.

"I-yah-bide-yah side-by-side-yah with-da-king, he was a lion," he continued in his sing-song chant.

The three students practically clambered over each other to assail the baboon with questions:

"Wow! A real lion king?"

"What was he like?"

"Was he big?"

The baboon turned one eye from his trinkets toward them as if they were asking something simple, that they didn't realize was simple. "A lion-here-a lion-there-yah what-sa difference anywhere-yah?"

"No, I mean, what was he like?"

"Was he horrible like we hear in school?"

"Hoo, hoo! Horr-ee-bul you just might find-ah in the looky person eye-ah!" The baboon waved a stick bedecked with innumerable bits of jungle ennui that rattled.

"What is that supposed to mean?"

The teacher purred, "I think he's saying that something—like the lion king, for example—can be good or bad depending on the viewpoint of the animal seeing or encountering it. Can you tell us what makes you say that, sir?"

"Hooma-hi-yah, can't deny-yah: WE GEDDALL DAH NICE-AH THINGS-AH, WHEN WE'RE CLOSE-AH TO THE KING-ZAH!"

Prince asked, "So, for a lion king's assistant like you, and for the king and his family and friends, for them you're saying that it was pretty good?"

The eccentric old baboon suddenly dropped all his amulets and leapt directly in front of Prince, grinning an enormous gold-filled grin and jabbing his long, bony finger at the cub's chest. "BINGO!"

XLIV

AFTER Prince and his classmates had enjoyed special experiences related to the Animal Farm and Old Country lion kings, other teachers introduced them to visiting creatures from animal zoos around the world. They were able to learn similarities and differences compared against their own animal zoo from respected experts. But what they really wanted—and felt ready for—was some firsthand, practical experience ... in leading.

"Let's go, let's go! Keep up, you three," the still-young cheetah called over his shoulder to his students trying valiantly to catch up with him. When planning an intense, hands-on learning opportunity, he often took his classes out to remote areas of the gardens where there were fewer distractions.

For this lesson, the cubs would practice being leaders. They began by making speeches for selection. Their speeches were nearly identical, and each could be summarized roughly with, "You should select me as leader, because I have lots of good ideas for making our class better." Actually, these speeches were no more vague or immeasurable than the leader speeches given by actual leaders wooing voters for selection.

The first learning opportunity came when the selection vote was a draw. It seems each student had voted for himself. After briefly permitting his three pupils to argue about the best solution for this impasse, Mr. Bolt finally stepped in. "Since each of you is convinced he'd be best as leader, none of you will ever vote for someone other than himself. So, why don't we simply let you take turns?"

The three young lions reluctantly agreed, eyeing each other with suspicion. After several unsuccessful attempts at picking an order, Mr. Bolt recommended they cast lots, and the three again reluctantly agreed, eyeing each other with suspicion.

The exercise was trying. Each cub was convinced that he was best qualified to lead, and that he had the best ideas and plans for the position. None of them had the remotest interest in playing the role of follower when their turn came.

At last the exercises came to an end and Mr. Bolt gathered them for conclusory thoughts. Each cub shared something he'd learned. Finally, Mr. Bolt closed, "Now you see the importance of your studies, as well as your family resources and connections, because once you've had a taste of leadership, you'll never be satisfied hanging around with the rest of the pack anymore!"

On that note, Mr. Bolt exploded in a flash of yellow and black, shooting like lightning from the remote outdoor classroom back to the school with three eager young lion cubs panting away in a futile attempt to keep up.

BOOK EIGHT
CODY

XLV

CODY the capybara was missing. At first his mother simply assumed he was somewhere amongst the pack of her little capybaras that were constantly running and bouncing all around her. However, once she got them all still and drifting off to sleep, she found she was one little capybara short. Even this problem failed to induce panic, since so many young animals in the neighborhood played together and visited in one another's homes. She thought Cody must have lost track of time at a friend's house. Surely he'd return shortly.

Only he didn't.

When he continued not returning, his mother began to check with his friend's mothers. None of them had seen him all day. Her anxiety began to rise.

Next, Cody's mother went to see Rockie, his school teacher. Although it was quite late, Rockie was not asleep. She was a post-middle-aged raccoon who stayed up most of the night. When Rockie told Cody's mother that her son hadn't been at school all day, her panic became full-blown. She unleashed her anger and fear on the nearest target.

"What do you mean he wasn't at school all day? Why didn't you contact me then? Did it ever cross your sleep-deprived mind that something might be wrong, you incompetent trash-eater?"

"Hey, I think you need to back off!" Rockie replied. "What kind of good-for-nothing mother doesn't know her child is missing 'til he's been gone a whole day? Maybe if you cared a little, you'd have noticed sooner, you over-grown guinea pig!"

What began with words, soon erupted into a physical fight, with claws flashing, teeth gleaming, and fur flying. A neighbor who heard the ruckus called the authorities. When they arrived and ascertained what was going on, they chided both animals for their foolhardy behavior. Precious time that could have been spent searching for Cody had been wasted. Neither Cody's mother nor his teacher was able to internalize what the peace officer was saying.

"Well, she started it, name-calling and accusifying people—"

"Me?! Oh, hell no, she-weakling! She started it with her late-night catting about—too tired to pay attention when her students don't show up for class! And not telling their parents—"

"Nobody's a parent for that boy! You don't even know where he was all day! Parent! Ha!"

At that remark, Cody's mother jumped at his teacher again, and the public safety officers were only able to separate them with the greatest effort. This delay detracted from the effort to search for little Cody.

XLVI

THE morning was not yet anything more than a dark, red-orange backdrop to the black tree silhouettes, but the inhabitants of those ominous black shapes were already astir. Birds were cackling the news of the night, and the hosts of the bird shows were gathering information. Soon the entire zoo was stretching itself to life, bleary-eyed, messy-haired, and funny smelling, preparing for the new day. No amount of stretching, scratching, or blinking, however, prepared anyone sufficiently for the shocking news that awaited: a young animal was missing.

The bird shows interviewed Cody's mother and his teacher Rockie, each of whom continued to heap accusations upon the other, to the extent that they failed to provide any information helpful for or pertinent to the search. Fortunately, the birds also interviewed public safety officers who gave a description of the missing youth.

"He stands under 18 inches tall, he has medium brown fur all over, no tail, and rodent-like facial features." Here a public safety sketch artist held up a picture that was so blotchy and smeared it could literally have been any animal in the gardens. "He should answer to the name 'Cody.' We are unsure at this time where he was last seen. If you have any information you believe would be helpful, please inform myself or any other public safety officer."

All that day information poured in, as each animal, with delusions of self-importance, figured he or she held the key to solving the mystery. The authorities were left to sort through the haystack of information seeking a needle of relevance.

"... There was a suspicious-looking wombat near the mini-train last week."

"... I saw a tuft of brownish hair in a macaw nest by the ice cream kiosk."

"... My rheumatism is flaring up, which only happens when someone's run away or when it might rain."

"... I saw Rockie fiddling around with something in a pool of water the other night."

"... One of the meerkats went missing four days ago and was replaced with an exact replica!"

"... I have a premonition that strange animals from outer space were involved."

"... I may have seen a little capybara around the playground equipment yesterday morning before school hours."

"... Perhaps he never was a capybara after all; probably just an overgrown guinea pig living among us who finally decided to go back home."

"... I've noticed Chester hanging around on the weakling bars at the playground the past few days."

"... I heard a funny voice behind the warthog enclosure yesterday evening, and then something smelled terrible!"

The authorities following up on various leads did stop to question Chester, a massive old Burmese python coiled up atop the weakling bars at the playground, but he stated that he didn't know anything about a missing capybara.

XLVII

THE parents of young animals attending school with Prince breathed a collective sigh of relief that tragedies like the disappearance of a young animal had not affected their side of the mini-train tracks. The parents of the students attending Mr. Slylock's school breathed a collective sigh of relief that it wasn't a young animal from their neighborhood. The parents of the young animals who attended Cody's school breathed a collective sigh of relief that the apparent tragedy, though involving a peer of their young, had not touched them directly.

Groups of animals from all these neighborhoods gathered at the main plaza and formed search parties to conduct passes through the zoo under the direction of public safety officers. Animals from Prince's neighborhood, mostly leaders who saw volunteer work as an opportunity to earn public support, posed magnificently. They gave speeches to encourage the actual searchers. Some appointed themselves to organize, or to distribute snacks and water to search party members. They were happy to be interviewed on the bird shows. Many were clever enough to be able to link the solution to the possible tragedy to some pet project or other. Many animals from Cody's neighborhood and the area around Mr. Slylock's school formed lines led by public safety officers and combed through sections of the zoological gardens, calling Cody's name and looking for clues. As they cleared each section, the group would return to the main plaza headquarters, where there was a giant, billboard-sized map of the gardens. Public safety officers used green-colored pins to identify sections on the map that had been cleared, and directed search parties to areas that still needed to be searched.

Chester did not participate in the searches. He remained wadded up in a massive coil on top of the weakling bars at the playground.

XLVIII

AS the days passed, fear and anxiety increased exponentially in Cody's mother as the hope of finding her son safe diminished. None of the animals felt comfortable openly expressing a lack of hope, though all felt it, for fear of becoming a pariah among all the other animals putting up the same false airs. Everyone, from bird show hosts to leaders to public safety officers to parents, everyone knew the likelihood of finding Cody safe was approaching zero, but they felt compelled by societal pressures to speak otherwise.

"... We at the office of public safety are confident that new developments are just around the corner, as we exhaust each key lead that might bring us closer to finding little Cody," frowned a serious-faced spokes-lynx, utilizing every facial muscle possible to de-emphasize his otherwise comical ear tufts.

"... And while this, our community of hope, continues to search for little Cody, we will maintain our commitment to bring you every update and keep—WHO?—keep you informed," the grim-faced owl suddenly brightened as she continued, "Phil—WHO?—Phil, do you have our weather-guess for today?"

Mothers chatting together over fences assured one another that "he'd turn up" and bewailed the tendency of their own young to constantly worry them. Fathers gave one another knowing nods over the drinking pools, and with a wink reminded each other that boys would be boys, and how they had all snuck around in their own youth and nothing bad had come of it.

Young animals began, with their infinite trust and carefree attitude, to forget all the cautions that had been pounded into them at both school and home lately. The scary dreams diminished, and little ones began roaming the zoo freely again, as if nothing had happened.

Schools, following the usual inexact mandate of the leaders, "took measures to prevent a similar occurrence in the future." Teachers were required to maintain a written roll tally of students by asking each one individually if he or she was, in fact, present. They had to show the tally to any parent who requested to see it within at least three weeks of the request. Had it been in place, this measure would have had absolutely no impact on either Cody's disappearance or the delay discovering it. Leaders, nonetheless, joined school administrators in praising the changes as monumental. They assured parents that these measures were a "great step" toward ensuring the safety of all students.

If only they had been right.

XLIX

THE guinea fowl came streaming willy-nilly into the main plaza of the zoo, shrieking as though the sky was—right that very minute—in the process of violently falling. At first, this behavior elicited a negligible response from the other animals because the guinea fowl had an annoying tendency to both run willy-nilly, and to shriek the world's pending doom when nothing remotely earth-shattering had occurred. Once the animals found out what had excited the guineas this time, however, they all got excited as well. Foraging near the playground, the guinea fowl had spotted Chester trying to eat a young gorilla.

A crowd of animals surrounded the weakling bars, on top of which Chester still lay curled. A visibly shaken little gorilla sat at the bottom of the weakling bars hugging his knees tightly.

" … great big fusssss over nothing, I assssure you. I offered a piece of candy to little DK here, and he sssseemed to be choking. Isssn't that right, DK? SSSo, I tried to help him ssspit the candy out. Perhapsss that isss what thossse bird-brained busssy bodiesss sssaw."

"Well?" the public safety officer turned to the flock of guinea fowl. "Did you actually see Chester try to eat DK?"

"He was wrapped around him—REEEE!—"

"And squeezing! REEEE!—"

"And his—REEE—mouth was open—"

"REEEE!"

"His mouth was open! REEEE!—"

"REEE! Moving toward the little—REEE—gorilla's head!"

"Yep! REEEE! Towards his head!"

"—didn't see any candy—"

"Nope! REEEE! No candy—REEE!"

The public safety officer, a brawny grizzly bear, hunched down trying to bring himself level with DK. "Can you tell me what happened, little fella?"

In silence, DK turned white-rimmed eyes back and forth between Chester and the officer.

"Did the python offer you some candy?"

Up-and-down went the small, thick gorilla head. "Did you take the candy?"

Up-and-down.

"Did you choke on the candy?"

Glance up at Chester. Glance down at feet. Glance back up at Chester. Begin rocking slightly.

"That might be a tough question. Why don't I let you think about it while I ask some other animals questions—would that be okay?"

Up-and-down.

The officer stood up. "Chester, I'm going to need you to come down so we can talk about this. I'm not talking to you up on these weakling bars. Come on down now."

Slowly the massive python began unraveling, various coils of his body appearing to go one way while others went another. All at once, a collective gasp arose from the crowd of animals gathered at the playground. There, in the middle of Chester's great bulk, was a pronounced lump, a lump approximately the size of a young capybara.

L

THE entire zoo population was in a state of uproar. The news spread like wildfire that Chester appeared to have eaten young Cody and was seeking a second victim in DK. In every quarter has was presumed guilty and vilified as a monster.

"They shouldn't even wait for a determination by the magistrates, they should skin him alive!"

"Don't be a fool! That wouldn't be enough, after all, snakes regularly skin themselves ..."

"They ought to put that monster into the grinder that makes dingo food—tail first!"

"Didn't your uncle Milt get hung in that grinder?"

"Just awful! That's why he's got the missing foreleg, you know. Worst thing that could ever happen to an animal, and the perfect thing for that beast!"

"The question AWWWK! that everyone around this zoo is asking, Woodsey," the parrot on one bird show shrugged at the owl beside her, "is why? AWWWWK!"

"WHO?"

"Everybody, AWWWK! They wonder why any creature in our advanced society AWWWK! would descend so low as to do this to our young."

"WHO?"

"Our young, AWWK! Why would Chester do this?"

"WHO?"

"Chester. Look, we all have AWWK! urges sometimes, but that is the true mark of civilized society AWWWK! to overcome urges that injure self or others. Without that, we are no better than the weaks!"

"WHO?"

"It's sick, that's what it is. Just sick. He sat there on those dumb bars watching all of us searching our paws to the bone, hunting everywhere, with him knowing the whole time where that poor little capybara was—"

"Disgusting!" spat another mother leaning on the fence at the meeting of four yards.

"Filthy reptile," shuddered a third, "not even real animals, I say."

"The thing is," rejoined the first, "he didn't learn anything. He was just going to keep doing this again and again. This thing with the little gorilla proves that. There's just no cure for someone like that."

But no one would ever know if there was a cure for Chester in particular. In the cage where he was awaiting his turn before the magistrates, he made himself into a noose and hung himself.

BOOK NINE

METRO

AND

BERSERKR

LI

O F course, an event of the magnitude of Chester's now-uncovered misdeeds and his untimely demise brought waves of excitement: leader appearances, bird show antics, and magisterial commentary. A perfect environment existed for snatching attention, and the attention snatchers were ready.

While Gordo was pompously postulating to crowds about the occurrences surrounding Chester, a murmur started like a ripple in the back of the audience. Animals parted leaving a path and then slowly resumed their former places as the yet unknown thing moved through the masses. At last the thing drew close enough to the front where Gordo stood that he and the information gatherers from the bird shows could see it plainly. It was a march. A two-animal march.

The two-animal march that had usurped Gordo's attention began to stomp emphatically in an oval-shaped path in the open space vacated by the birds immediately in front of him. Metro, a meticulous porcupine, carried a sign that read, "HAPPY RIGHTS" displayed very artistically on a flowered background. Beserkr, a temperamental Tasmanian devil, carried one that read, "YOU CAN'T BEAT US, SO JOIN US!" as he circled opposite Metro. Soon the two began a call-and-respond chant.

"I DO"

"WHAT I WANT"

"I DO"

"WHAT I WANT"

"I DO"

"WHAT I WANT"

The information gatherers for the bird shows often missed the forest for the trees. In this instance, for example, they were so absorbed by the two-animal march and how serious and even ominous the airs adopted by Metro and Berserkr were that they missed the poor choice of phrases to chant. "I do what I want" was the universal mantra of barely weaned baby animals asserting their infantile independence. It was hardly appropriate or ideal as a phrase defining the cause of mature animals desiring to make a portentous statement. Oblivious to the irony, the birds completely forgot Gordo and quickly gathered around the oval formed by the marching pair.

"What are you marching for? Or is it against?"

"Can you explain the statement your movement is trying to make?"

"What are 'Happy Rights'?"

Ignoring these questions, Metro and Berserkr broke from their oval march, followed each other single file, and stopped just in front of the erstwhile significant Gordo, facing the birds.

Metro raised his hands delicately—as if the birds facing him were full of needle sharp quills pointing at him rather than the other way around, and the crowd quieted down for him to speak.

LII

METRO, whose quills were arranged stylishly and glistened slightly with fragrant oil, spoke with an almost imperceptible hint of a lisp. "Well, we certainly have lots of questions, don't we? That's nice. In case you didn't know, I'm Metro," he said turning both dainty paws inward to rest together on his soft, quill-less chest. "And this," he gestured to his right, "is Berserkr."

"You ask what we're marching for, so, we're marching for Happy Rights. Berserkr and I are happy when we're together, and we believe we have the right to be happy and the right to be together. We have the right to live in our own enclosure, rather than in the porcupine and Tasmanian devil habitats, respectively; isn't that right, Berserkr?" Metro's paw bent down gently onto his twitchy little associate's shoulder.

Berserkr twitched and grunted in what all present presumed to be an affirmative response.

"So, you see," continued Metro, "if porcupines who choose to live with porcupines have their own enclosure, and Tasmanian devils who choose to live with Tasmanian devils have their own enclosure, then porcupines who choose to live with Tasmanian devils should not be treated any differently. We want to be able to share food and water and bedding and habitat like everyone else. Yay! I mean, it's not like we're hurting anyone, right?"

With that said, Metro and Berserkr took up their signs and marched back through the crowd that separated to accommodate them, chanting as they went.

"I DO"

"WHAT I WANT"

"I DO"

"WHAT I WANT"

"I DO"

"WHAT I WANT"

In their wake, they left mayhem and confusion. Animals in the gardens had always been more or less free to associate as they pleased, and so they did. The enclosures, however, were arranged so that animals habituated, ate, drank, and slept among their kind. Now that a different way of thinking had been presented in such a public forum, debate sprang up all over the zoo.

LIII

THE bird shows predominantly favored Happy Rights, while the leaders predominantly favored whomever they believed could provide them the greatest chance at being selected again. Shrink and Quack were divided.

Shrink and Quack were a pair of flabby old walruses who were for the minds of the animals in the zoo what doctors Chip and Dale were for their bodies. Only not quite. It was easy for the doctors to see when a limb was broken or when someone had an infection or injury. Wounds or diseases of the mind were largely inexact and diagnosing them was, as a result, highly speculative.

For the entire storied length of the Animal Zoo—the same as the Animal Farm and the Old Country for that matter—an issue like Metro and Berserkr's would have been treated as an ailment of the mind by the contemporary equivalents of Shrink and Quack. That was about to change, however.

"Flabba, flabba, flabba!" exclaimed Shrink, shaking all the jowly blubber around his ivory tusks. "You have to agree that it is unnatural, then it must be a disease of the mind, Quack! Flabba, flabba, flabba!"

"Harummm, harumm!" retorted Quack, in like manner, "what is natural or unnatural must—harumm—must be viewed on an individual basis! You eat herring, which I find common and fishy. I prefer nice, clean shellfish, lightly smoked, if you please. Harrumm, yet just because we like different things doesn't make one of us diseased or ill, harrummm!"

"Flabba, flabba, flabba! We both still live in the walrus habitat, whether we eat the exact same food or not! Flabba, flabba. They aren't talking about eating different things or even preferring different foods, flabba, flabba, flabba. They're talking about cohabitating as if they were matched normally and naturally. If we use your eating example, it would be more like you choosing all of a sudden to consume nothing but bamboo shoots. They don't grow where we're from or in our habitat, they aren't suited to our teeth or digestive system. In short, flabba, flabba, flabba, there's something amiss with a walrus drawn to bamboo, and there's something equally amiss with a porcupine drawn to a Tasmanian devil!"

"Harrumm! Harrumm! Now an animal is injured or diseased in the mind for desiring something you deem inappropriate? Harumm! Harumm!"

No matter how long the two shifted and shook, jowls flying, no matter how their flippers flipped or tusks flashed, they could not come to an agreement. The very respectability of their profession was in jeopardy: who could trust the diagnosis of 'scientists' who couldn't even agree amongst themselves about a simple fact?

At long last, they decided to determine the science of the matter based on a vote. Unfortunately, when the ballots were tallied, they resulted in a 1-1 tie: one for Metro and Berserkr having a mental disease or defect, and one against. Several arguments ensued regarding the most optimal method for breaking the tie, until one proposed a weighted vote. Both Shrink and Quack agreed this was the most prudent option, so away to the scales they went. As it turned out, Quack was a bit more portly than Shrink, so the vote went his way. Metro and Berserkr and anyone like them were found by the Mind Association of Doctors, or MAD for short, to be perfectly healthy and sound, by an incontrovertible 60% to 40% margin.

LIV

THROUGHOUT the zoo it became socially unacceptable to make any comment that could be in any way loosely construed antagonistic to Metro and Berserkr's cause. Any such comment had to be carefully bookended with apparent unilateral support for them.

"Of course, I support what they're trying to do—we all want to be free to do what makes us happy," one bold but anonymous skeptic began. "I'm just concerned for what's best for the zoo. We all know how Berserkr is a light sleeper and very volatile. What happens if some of Metro's quills give him a fright in his sleep? He'll go on a whirlwind tour of the zoo—spinning and growling and zinging around—destroying anything in his path! Not that I hold that against them, it's just a danger."

"Oh, I agree," concurred a second skeptic who wished to have his name held in confidence. "I wouldn't be the one to keep anyone from what makes them happy, but think of the little ones! How can you ever teach them the way things are, what's supposed to be, if someone's forever going against the way things are? They'll be learning all kinds of craziness! Not that I mean Metro and Berserkr would do that, of course."

"Or—though the Happies should have rights—what do you say when your little ones start asking questions," rejoined the first. "For example, when they ask why Chester was wrong— he was just doing what he wanted, after all, right? Wonder what Ol' Shrink and Quack have to say about that? Not that I don't support Metro and Berserkr, naturally."

LV

METRO and Berserkr had brought so much attention to their cause with the public march and statement, and there had been so much discussion of the issue from MAD to the bird shows to schools to individual animals, that the leaders decided a special vote should be held. The vote would decide whether zoo animals would be permitted to habituate as they pleased, or grouped in their enclosures by families of like animals as previously.

Most animals experienced a positive feeling concerning the vote. After all, voting was so integral to the history of the zoo —it served as the foundation of equality that all animals had a say in how the zoo operated. In this instance, the secret ballot was also comforting. It permitted animals to vote as they felt right, despite the social stigma connected with opposing Metro and Berserkr's cause.

At last the highly anticipated day arrived. The whole zoo turned out for the event. Long lines snaked out of voting places as the animals exercised their right to control the operation of their zoo. Leaders' assistants carried ballot boxes to the central plaza where the votes were counted by a clever horse visiting the zoo from a traveling circus show. When the final votes had been tallied, the voting commissioner took his place before the anxious crowds to make his announcement.

"The votes have all been counted. The measure sponsored by Metro and Berserkr, the measure to extend enclosure right to animals of different species ... failed. Enclosures will continue to be held as they have been. The animals have spoken."

LVI

TRUE, Gordo was the Chief Magistrate. But there was an entity in the zoo so august that even he paled into insignificance before it. It was the Supreme Oracle.

The Supreme Oracle—whose members referred to themselves as The Trinity, interestingly enough—consisted of three individual Oracles, each one an animal who had served as a magistrate, and who had been chosen from among his or her peers. They were chosen for life, and no amount of misbehavior or poor decision-making or wrong action could be used to unseat them. A new member was chosen to join the Supreme Oracle only when his predecessor had literally predeceased him. When that occurred, the reigning lordmayor chose a replacement.

The Oracles were rarely seen in public and had no dealing with the other animals. They were wrinkled, crusty, old felines who never understood regular animals, and had long forgotten even the ways of the great cats among whom they'd once lived. The Supreme Oracle conducted its business in the Inner Sanctum, a small clearing behind a maintenance shed where paint thinner and diesel fuel had been disposed of until they had saturated the soil and their fumes permeated the entire area.

The three Oracles consisted of a lion, a tiger, and a panther. The lion, Nero, insisted on sitting in a throne-shaped chair and focused his scattered thoughts primarily on whether his tail should drape sideways over one of the armrests, forward over the seat, or straight up behind him along the seat back.

He fidgeted and squirmed and barked gummy remonstrances at his tail, oblivious to any proceedings underway.

The tiger, Crito, spent his days before a cracked and hazy old mirror twisting and contorting his arthritic carcass in a vain attempt to present a view of his multicolored coat in which the mangy bald spots could not be seen. The only other concern in his doddering, addled old brain—probably linked to how different the tiger's coat is from other cats—was to always contradict the opinions of the other two or in some way to clog up their machinations.

The panther, Token, had been picked by a lordmayor trying to ease light-dark tensions in the zoo, rather than for any sort of competence as a magistrate. He paced back and forth unceasingly blinking his rheumy, old, cataract-blinded eyes in the paint thinner and diesel fumes. Every few steps he would slurp at the chemical-induced drool streamers that perpetually hung from his gaping toothless jaw.

The founders of the Animal Zoological Gardens of Eden established the Supreme Oracle to keep the zoo true to the founding charter. The Supreme Oracle was to be the keeper of those ideals the zoo was founded upon by making decisions consistent with them. In practice, the Oracles were unable to refer to the charter, because they had long since ripped it up for use in their litter box. They made determinations in the zoo regarding whatever they wanted, and using whatever logic or lack thereof struck them. A large number of questions were raised to them over time, but they only considered ones they chose. Petitioners would present a question to the minions of the Oracles, who would generally refuse the question a number of times as unintelligible, improperly worded, insignificant, or in some other way unworthy of troubling the Oracles. Once the question fit the minions' exacting standards, they would place it on a silver tray and stand quietly before the Oracles with it until recognized. IF any of the individual Oracles happened to wave a paw while the minion stood waiting, it was taken as a sign that the Supreme Oracle was refusing to consider that question. That was the fate of 99.995% of questions presented by the minions in the Inner Sanctum. But every once in a great while ...

LVII

METRO and Bersekr were not to be deterred by something like the majority decision of the animals of the zoo. They presented their issue to the minions of the Supreme Oracle.

The minions, by no means afraid of any animal, their position being nearly as impregnable as that of the Oracles themselves, nonetheless bent to the contemporary chic and did nothing to oppose the question. They silver-trayed it and one carried it in great ceremony into the Inner Sanctum. None of the Oracles waved it away.

The minion who carried the question placed silver tray and all on a squat stump behind the maintenance shed. He then took a couple of steps back, stood reverently, head bowed, observing all.

"Doopid dail!" gummed Nero, swiping at his tail with a gnarled and clawless paw as the tail popped and cracked, dodging his efforts to switch it from one armrest to the other manually. "Tang dabbit! Gol' Durrit!" He inched down from his throne in slow motion, his joints a percussion symphony, staggered and fell face-first into the solvent-smelling dirt.

The minion hesitated, unsure if he should offer assistance, as Nero's breathing seemed to have hitched; but, his frame swelled a bit as he snuffed up the fumes oozing from the soil as greedily as his broken body could.

Meanwhile, Token's gouty pacing had not abated in the least. He criss-crossed back and forth over Nero's inert form, at each pass leaving the lowermost portions of his brace of drool streamers plastered across the matted hair of Nero's dull, lifeless mane.

"Color-iss muvvukkas!—slurp—Bline ol' pamfuh cane ged no nuttin' fum 'em color-iss muvvas. Aw 'bout dem lite cullas—slurp—lite cullas ged ebby thang—slurp—po' ol' bline pamfuh godda work dem ol' paws to day bones—slurp—Kwessions, kwessions!—slurp—'Yes, massuh!', 'No, massuh!', 'Boss, doan ritely know dat, massuh!'—slurp—Aw day, ebby day!"

Eventually, Nero dragged himself back over to his throne chair. He held his tail, curiously eyeing it as if he wasn't sure where it had come from.

"Doopit, uh, whadda yoo think dis here is? Doopit SOMEthing! Whaddo I do widdit when I siddown? Doopid dwession. Too hard. Asss diff'unt dwession. Doan like that dwession."

Crito frowned and untwisted himself from before his mirror. He hobbled over to the contaminated dirt and inhaled deeply several times, each time following his inhale with a raspy, sneeze-ish exhale.

"Norange, mlack, white, mlack, white, norange, white, norange, mlack, mmm, ssss SNERT sss."

He hobbled and swayed on his rickety bird legs back over to his mirror, attempting to primp his mangy fur all the while.

"Doopit dail! Tang blabbin' doopit dail!"

"Color-iss muvvakkas! Lite cullas ged ebby-thang! Slurp!"

"Norange, mlack, white ... "

The minion, having thus heard and assimilated the grand decision of the Supreme Oracle, bowed slightly, retrieved the silver tray, and backed humbly from the Inner Sanctum. Among the other minions, he unfolded the scrap of paper bearing the query, and decorously penned his interpretation of the Oracles' answer below. He then returned outside to the waiting crowds, and with fitting pomp and circumstance, read the answer.

BOOK TEN

THOMAS

LVIII

"I'M even more confused than I was before Ol' Sly started trying to explain the Supreme Oracle's decision," Hope told her friends as they shuffled along after school. She kicked a pebble and sent it skittering along the dusty path ahead of them.

"Do you think he's going to make us explain all that on a test?" Caspar moaned as he kicked the small rock forward again.

"I hope not, because his explanation made no sense to me." Faith wasn't paying attention and stepped over the rock.

"Well, Faith, heh, heh, heh, maybe if you make up an answer that makes no sense, he'll count it as right!" Risa's laugh didn't even sound very enthusiastic, and he dejectedly kicked the small stone forward again.

"I for one," said Charity, clinging to Faith's neck and entirely ignoring the pebble below, "would really just like to understand. To me that's more important than Ol' Sly's test."

"Maybe Grandpa Tom could help us make heads or tails of it," suggested Hope, who accidentally kicked the rock a little too hard and sent it careening off the path. "Dang it!"

The little animals continued dragging along in the direction of the ancient tortoise's enclosure. They were tired from a long day of school, on top of having endured another of Slylock's convoluted explanations. It was a perfect day for the slow pace of Old Thomas' company. And they were sure they'd find him at home. Old Tom wasn't much for roaming.

LIX

"MMM, to be sure, you little scamps sure are always full of questions, aren't you?" Thomas was propped before a semicircle of little animals who had come to his enclosure straight from school; they were seeking straighter talk than they felt they got in class.

"We have to get answers somewhere, Grandpa Tom," Hope said.

"Well, maybe, as they say, this is as good a place as any to get answers, to be sure," the wizened old tortoise, for all his old and sometimes cranky airs, really did enjoy giving the little ones honest answers and understandable explanations, at times just to spite Old Slylock, if for no other reason. "Mmm, hmm. So what questions do you have today, as they say?"

"Well, you know how the Animal Zoo is supposed to be different from the Animal Farm and the Old Country?"

"Mmm."

"And how all animals are supposed to be equal?"

"Mmm."

"And how the votes of all animals are supposed to matter; how they're supposed to control how things operate in the gardens?"

"Mmm."

"And how that's supposed to be so much better and more fair than a lion king and his buddies deciding everything and forcing it on everyone else?"

"Mmm."

At this point, Caspar had already had about enough of all Hope's preliminary interrogatives, and blurted, "So how come when the animals all voted against Metro and Berserkr's idea, how come it got changed by the Supreme Oracle against what all the animals chose? What's the point of saying the animals get to choose if they can't really choose any more than they could in the Old Country or in the animal farms?"

"Mmm, hmm ... yes. A good question, to be sure. Did you ask your teacher at school today?"

"Yes," Faith replied.

"Hardy, har, har. But his answer didn't seem very good," Risa added. "He said we had to have a Supreme Oracle because animals might make a wrong or stupid choice. He said the Supreme Oracle was there to make sure all the choices were right."

"Risa's right, Grandpa Tom, that's what Mr. Slylock said," Charity cooed. "But isn't that really the same as where someone else makes all the decisions anyway? Like the pigs in the animal farms or the lion kings in the Old Country? Like where there really isn't any vote, any freedom, or any equality?"

"Mmm, hmm ... very well ... mmm, hmm ... as they say ... to be sure ... hmm ..."

The young animals watched as Old Tom masticated at nothing and muttered to himself extensively. His face pointed upwards and his eyes squinted so severely they appeared to be shut entirely. The little ones hesitated to interrupt whatever it was that he had going on in his withered old head. But they were all pretty sure something was going on in there.

LX

OLD Thomas slowly began to emerge from the depths of his own thoughts, muttering, "Yes ... well ... to be sure ... mustn't be hasty ... as they say ... hmm ... So, as you say, it doesn't seem right that the free, equal animals of The Animal Zoological Gardens of Eden should have their choice reversed or overruled by three dilapidated old cats. Mmm, hmm. Is that about it?"

"Doesn't it mean we're not at all equal if those three Oracles have a vote that is more important than all the hundreds or even thousands of animals in the whole zoo?"

"Yes, to be sure, it certainly seems that way, Pumpkin." Old Tom's pet name for Hope only coincidentally fit the little pachyderm's round squat shape.

"Doesn't it make our Animal Zoo about the same as the animal farms where the pigs just tell all the animals what to do, and the animals have no say in anything?" asked Charity.

"Mmm, hmm ... it does seem to resemble those poor farms very closely, to be sure, Bunny." The old tortoise's nickname for Charity likely stemmed from her rabbit-like soft fur.

"And as I keep wondering," Faith shook her head, "why is it always great cats and their closest friends? Why no other animals? Isn't that almost the same as the Old Country?"

"Well, as you say, there certainly appears to be a similarity, Tater." No one could figure out where Old Tom got his pet name for Faith. "Have any of you ever thought to ask, as they say, a leader these questions? I mean, to be sure, one other

171

than Slylock, if you take him to be any sort of lesser leader ..."

"No, we never really see leaders close enough to ask them anything."

"They live pretty far off, and I don't think they let other animals into their area."

"Mmm, hmm. Well, as they say, to get to the bottom of a question, sometimes you have to go to the bottom!"

Though Thomas was able to infuse the little animals with some of his enthusiasm about getting to the bottom of their questions, they were at a complete loss for what he meant by going to the bottom.

LXI

O LD Thomas ponderously pulled himself across part of his enclosure to a small volcano-shaped mound of dirt with a hole in its top leading down into the earth. Snaking away from the mound in three of four directions were smaller horizontal mounds that suggested subterranean tunnels had been constructed leading who knew where.

"Hey there, mmm hmm, Morocco! Come out, as they say, you rascal!" Old Tom rasped at the central mound.

Nothing happened.

Old Tom did not seem too troubled by nothing happening, in fact, he seemed to be in his element.

Nothing continued happening, as the little animals became increasingly antsy, shifting feet, scratching, and watching passing insects.

Eventually, a soft scraping sound could be heard faintly coming from the dirt hole. The sounds grew louder and were accompanied by a low humming. The little animals looked at one another questioningly, but each shrugged ignorance of what to expect. Meanwhile, Old Tom was resting his head and wrinkly neck on the ground.

At last the brown furry head and pink star nose of a mole erupted out of the hole in the mound.

"Ah, Thomas! Jolly good show! Work, work, work, you see, always something busy busy! It's the same, busy with company, nose itching, all that rot, you know! Jack's a donut, but

173

that's a mighty glare! Mighty bright, I say, isn't it?" The mole blinked unremittingly.

"Morocco, to be sure, I know you're busy," Old Tom began, his head easing up from the ground where it rested, "what can you tell us—"

"News from the bottom is it, what? Yes, very good!—"

"What can you tell us specifically," continued Thomas, "about how to access the great cats and carnivores' area?"

"Oh, yes, well, tricky business, that! Ho! Jolly good, what? Tricky business indeed! Bit queer asking today and all that, isn't it? Queer, tricky business today, or my name's not Winthrop Peebles, you see? What?"

"But his name really isn't Winthrop Peebles, is it?" Faith whispered aside to Charity, who replied directly in Faith's ear:

"I don't think so, but it's hard to tell. He talks funny!"

"Heard that, little lady, dull eyes, keen ears, what? Says so in the book, doesn't it? Jolly queer, that! Ho!"

"But access to the carnivores, Morocco?" Thomas usually the first tangent chaser, drew the mole back.

"Ha! Pretty pickle, isn't it? Whole area closed off, tight as the drummer boy's snare. Closed for maintenance. Two-three days they say, if you please, or even if you don't! And there's the fix: sooner get at the crocodile's tongue. Ha! Jolly tight spot, what?"

"So there's no way to see them then? None at all, Mr. Morocco?" Hope's disappointment was equally evident in all her friends' faces.

"Step to there, missy! Never said that, little lady, bosh and stuff, indeed! Ha! Always a way—chin up, head high, that's a girl! Jolly spry, old sport!"

"Ho, ho, ho! But you said it's closed for maintenance."

"'Ho' said the hyena, bits and pieces, eh? Ha! That's the laugh, is it? Bright as the captain's knickers! Have a sit, all you there, on the lanky lass. Ha! Give us a wee spot—shade as sweet as tea at four! I'll give Ol' Tom the where-you-will! Up tidy there! Clean as the cat's pajamas, what?"

Risa, Hope, and Caspar awkwardly clambered for grips as they piled up Faith, who stepped slightly away from the hole, making a rather large sun screen to shade the mole and the old tortoise. The two whispered conspiratorially for a few moments before the mole—blinking even in the shade—waved cheerily and turned back down his tunnels.

"Tally ho, jolly good, what? Ol' Tom, as always, old fellow! Ha! Stuff and poppycock! Ho!" he cried as he vanished from sight.

LXII

IT didn't matter how anxious the young animals were to get where they were going, they could only go as fast as the slowest member of the group—Thomas—because he was the only one who knew where they were going. Morocco had whispered to him the directions to a secret observation point from which most of the great cats' area was clearly visible. So it didn't matter that the whole area was closed for maintenance; they were approaching using back paths and service gates.

As Thomas plodded along the way, the hyperactive little animals bounced like jumping beans all around him.

"How much farther, do you think, Grandpa Tom?"

"What do you think we'll see when we get there?"

They crept along the ground, or ran hiding-spot to hiding-spot like an assault party. They tiptoed and snuck like secret agents. They whispered and gestured signs to each other like spies.

Thomas, nonplussed, methodically dragged along, exactly one step at a time, no more.

At last, when the young animals had played out every variety of every game and role-playing scenario they could think of, and Old Thomas appeared to have lost every smidgen of momentum he may have had to begin with, they all rounded a corner in the thick hedge they'd been following and found what they'd been seeking all along: a clear, unobstructed view into the great cats' world.

LXIII

THE rise on which Thomas and the little animals found themselves did, in fact, overlook the great cat and carnivore world. However, the thick hedge they had followed continued in front of them and obscured much of the view for shorter animals like Thomas and Caspar. Risa could just peek over by standing on his hind legs and supporting himself against Hope's solid shoulder.

"Whoa!" Faith said, somewhere between an undertone and a whisper.

"Hardy, har, HAR!" agreed Risa.

"Mmm, hmm, to be sure, I've always wondered, as they say, why they're forever closing this area for maintenance. Now after all these years, I'm finally here to look in, as they say, and these bushes are in the way! Hmm! Tell me what you see, hmm."

"Well, Grandpa Tom, it's a lot," Hope said slowly. "There's lions and tigers and bears; there's leopards and cheetahs and lynxes; there's alligators and everything ..."

"Ho, ho, whoa! There's Gordo and Snivel and Diablo and the rest of the howler monkeys!" Risa continued. "Leaders and sub-leaders and assistants and deputies and whatever else ..."

"I think that's the Supreme Oracles over behind that building over there," added Charity.

"Mmm hmm, but what else? As you say, is there anything else that would explain the closing of the area?"

"Lots and lots of thrones. Thrones EVERYwhere," Faith drawled. "Thrones of ivory, thrones of bones, thrones covered in all kinds of animal skins and pelts. Thrones decorated with teeth and bones. Thrones and thrones and thrones ... there must be as many thrones as animals down there ..."

"Hum, hum, hum. And crowns ... I can't see any animal down there anywhere without a crown, heh, heh, heh. Thin ones, thick ones, all colors and sizes, plain ones, ornate ones ... Not just lions or leaders either: every animal down there has a crown."

"Dancing and singing," Charity cooed almost too softly to hear. "Dancing and singing around those fires there ... Huge groups singing and dancing and circling those fires ..."

Caspar had been frantically pacing back and forth impatient for his friends to describe the scenes below. His strong sense of smell told him a meal was afoot, and he could bear the suspense no longer. He sprang onto the top of Old Thomas' shell and peered over the hedge into the closed section of the zoo.

"As an expert in all areas of food and eating, I must say, that is a feast! A gigantic barbecue feast," he reported.

Thomas' deep set old eyes widened perceptibly and he moved and spoke with a novel sense of urgency, "Come, children! Come! To be sure, it is time for us to go, now!"

"Bar-be-cue? Barbecue what, Caspar?"

"Can't quite tell. Unfamiliar to me," Caspar snuffed loudly with his snout to the sky. "Not a usual odor—"

"To be sure! Time to GO! Mmm hmm, we must leave now little friends! We have seen what we came to see! The leaders, the carnivores, the lions, as you say, they live differently. We have seen it, and we must go!" Thomas had already turned to retreat, and Caspar had to scamper around the top of the time-worn shell and hop little hops to stay facing the feast.

"What are all those little shapes in the fire?" asked Faith, straining her long neck and squinting into the bright flames.

"Please, children! Mmm hmm, you must come away from there!" Thomas raced away at his top speed, barely noticeably faster than his normal speed.

"Are they ... animal-shaped ... only smaller?" Hope peered.

"NO, NO, NO!" for once Risa didn't laugh. "Little animals —collections! That's a whole world of kings, worse than the animal farms' pigs! A world of kings feasting on all the zoo's babies!"

Thomas stopped racing. Caspar stopped hopping. Charity climbed down from Faith's neck and began to crawl along the ground away from the sight. Hope wept salty tears that began eroding wrinkles around her huge, dark eyes. Faith turned to be sick over the hedge beside her.

From a distance, casual observers would have believed they saw six very old, decrepit animals moving painfully back along the maintenance roads and service paths behind public areas of the Animal Zoological Gardens of Eden.

AFTERWORD

I have always enjoyed George Orwell's *Animal Farm*, and wondered—perhaps with many of you—why didn't those animals ever get it? And the real question, why didn't the Russian people get how they were duped all these years? Orwell's brilliance in making his allegory fun, historically relevant, and gripping touches me viscerally.

For almost thirty years, I read *Animal Farm* and pondered the possibility of a similar allegory illuminating the duping I perceive in the changes that have occurred since the earliest days and ideals of the United States. I wrote several initial paragraphs. I had a few ideas scrawled on misshapen bits of scrap paper and restaurant napkins, though it is beyond me where any of these could be found today.

At one point during my incarceration, the Jesus-followers with whom I surrounded myself and I were in a period of reflection on hearing God's call through Holy Spirit "nudges" to our own spirits; we were trying to be open to His voice. We were also trying to remove a lot of the "self" that takes ideas and plots and plans and overworks and fills restaurant napkins with illegible scrawling and sketches. We were trying to be subject to God's plans. In me, this manifested in a feeling that if God intended for me to write this book, He would make it happen; but if not, it wouldn't.

This spirit-walking attitude gives a whole new approach to what could otherwise be burdensome or anxiety-plagued. I determined that I would simply sit down and write the book.

No plotting. No planning. No outlining or mapping. I would just write as much as I felt, as I felt it, without stopping.

I wrote the rough draft in two days in an illegible cursive and print jumble on loose-leaf paper, with arrows to position add-ins scrabbled all over the backs of the pages. For the next few days, I tried to read what I had written and rewrite it legibly. Then I left it. I was done.

The only significant rewrite is the ending, from about chapter 58 to the conclusion of the book. The original ending, which some will find entertaining despite its change in focus, is available on request.

Eventually, I was transferred to an institution that afforded me the opportunity to type the manuscript. For some proofreading I wanted and publication, I needed an electronic version. I sat in a public library upon my release from prison and typed this story and was floored by what I found. There was so much I didn't remember writing. There were so many little pieces that add so much to the allegory, that point to ills of humanity and our society. There was so much that didn't come from me. I truly believe God is sharing this story with America. I'm just a simple fella. I didn't have this much story in me.

Another thing I found upon release was a drastic decrease in the acceptability of serious discussion in our culture. We've always joked about avoiding religion and politics at family gatherings, but this has gone from joke to world view. Friendships end, conversation becomes violent, and families disrupt over differing opinions. In contrast, an Israeli friend of mine tells me the witticism in Israel is that if you have a gathering of family and friends, you'd better talk about religion and politics!

The important takeaway I want readers to have with *Animal Zoo* is not unilateral acceptance of my opinions. In fact, in many ways I've tried to mask which side of issues I land on. I only intend to illuminate some issues, share some good logic and expose some bad, and facilitate discussion. Relationship is the key. Relationship comes from discussion, not dictation. Relationship grows with listening more than talking.

My opinion is that some of the issues, if treated as one side wants to, are quite detrimental for our society. But the inability to listen and discuss both sides of issues as mature, intelligent, caring people spells a much more threatening doom for the future of respectable society.

A NOTE ABOUT INDIE PUBLISHING

Word-of-mouth is crucial for any author to succeed. Even more so in the world of Independent Publishing. If you enjoyed Animal Zoo please leave a review online—anywhere you are able, Amazon, Goodreads, Bookbug, BookTok. Even if it's just a sentence or two.

I can't tell you how much I personally appreciate you taking the time to share your feedback. I'm sure it will help other readers find something they enjoy!

Thank you!

Orso Marrone

MEET THE AUTHOR

Orso Marrone developed the ideas found in Animal Zoo over the course of decades. Most of that time, lots of development wasn't happening. Then, in a crazy burst of writing frenzy, lots of development happened in two days.

Those two days were spent in a prison cell in Petersburg, VA. They occurred approximately ten years into Orso's time incarcerated. He wrote this story and performed the first several edits by hand.

During the years following Orso's ill-fated court-martial, he wrote prolifically. Follow his author page to see what to expect as he works frantically to publish handwritten stories, drawings on napkins, children's books, and poetry written while looking through the dungeon's barred windows for your enjoyment and elucidation.

https://barrybrown.art/the-nom-de-guerre

ALL OF THE OTHER REINDEER

DO THESE SHORTS MAKE ME LOOK FAT?

COMING SOON!

ALL OF THE OTHER REINDEER

In time for Christmas, release in August 2026! You know the story of Rudolph, but how did Santa Claus come to have Dasher, or Dancer, or Prancer, or Vixen? Not to mention Comet or Cupid, much less Donner or Blitzen. You have no idea, because the legend has never been recorded since the dawn of time! UNTIL NOW that is! The entire story of Santa, the elves, Missus Claus, and the eight reindeer besides Rudolph, written and illustrated by Orso Marrone in the chow hall at the military prison at Fort Leavenworth.

DO THESE SHORTS MAKE ME LOOK PHAT?

Award-winning short stories by Barry Brown. Many genres, many lengths. Westerns, romance, sci-fi, memoir, flash fiction, holiday stories, fantasy, and stories defying categorization.

The only thing tying these stories together is judges loved them all! Well, that and they were written by the same guy.